WHERE LOVE RESIDES

To Jasmine
Thank you so much
for sharing your light
+ gift with us.
Peace + Blessings
— Ashley A.T.

WHERE LOVE RESIDES

By Ashley A.T.

Where Love Resides

Copyright © 2019 Ashley A.T.

ISBN: 978-1-7731336-0-9

Edited by Carol Gaskin
Cover by OliviaProDesign

Of The Ash Tree Publishing, LLC.
www.ashley-at.com

DEDICATED TO

All of the lives lost, mourned, and not-forgotten because of police brutality in America.

Thank you.
-Ashley

"Death doesn't end a life if we don't let it. A man only dies when the living forget his legacy."

Prologue

Time is a web of events, a pattern of significant points connected by the thread of passing moments, that all lead to one big something. There are times in our lives, just as some monumental life event is about to occur, when we stop to look back at this web of Life and reflect on what's led us here.

Gabe Mathis is having such a moment. Months after the Curse of the Red Sea fell upon New Locale, and Gabe and Chanel are sitting in Dr. Rhen's office, waiting to learn the sex of their unborn child. Silence fills the exam room as Gabe gazes quietly out the window. His cellphone rings.

"Hello," he answers with a calm voice.

"What's good bro?" An exuberant young man's voice asks from the other end.

"Hey, bro. Can I call you back?" Gabe responds. "I'm a little busy with Cha for her checkup."

"Oh! Is it *the* checkup?" The person on the line asks.

"Yeah, *that* checkup." He laughs.

"Word! Get back to me with the big news! I'll be at the TM Center when you're done."

"All right, cool. We'll meet you out there in a few. Be easy."

He slides down in his chair a little and looks outside, contemplating. Sitting up on the bed, dressed in a hospital gown, Chanel asks, "Was that your brother?"

"He's already calling himself 'Uncle Marcus,'" Gabe says smiling as he shakes his head. "Waiting to see if he's having a niece or nephew. He's excited for real though."

His smile fades as he goes back into deep thought. Chanel examines his expression for a bit, then with the same sort of solemnness, she looks down, staring at her bare feet, thinking of what to say.

"I can't tell if you share the same excitement as him," she comments, tilting her head up slightly to watch his response.

"*Oh!* Yeah, babe. You know I do," he says. Wide-eyed, his expression changes to ease the state of uncertainty he's placed on them both. "How could I not be? I'm just thinking…" he trails off.

"You're afraid?"

"Scared of the unknown, I guess. Like, in a couple of months, I'm for real going to be someone's father! Am I even ready?" He leans over in his chair, holding his head up with his hands. "I don't want him, or her, to be hardened by the world the way I was, you know? Plus the city has been upside-down lately. I've been here my whole life and I barely recognize it now. Is this the right place for us to be? Do we have enough to get out if things go back to how they were before—"

Chanel throws her head back as a great laugh escapes before she covers her mouth to catch herself. Gabe glares at her with his eyebrow raised, his mouth still open from her interruption.

"I'm sorry, but you so caught me off guard," she says, still giggling. "Like, who is this 'Worry Wart Gabe' and what have you done with my always right, know-it-all husband?"

There's a mirror on the wall in front of him, and as he catches a glimpse of himself, looking confused and disheveled, a smile lights across his face.

"You know," he starts, with the coolness in his voice returned. "You might be right, for once. The baby is changing us. I'm supposed to be the one who's solid, while you run through the unrealistic thoughts in your head."

"I know!" She shoots him a confident grin. "You're rubbing off on me," she admits.

He gets up to walk over to her. "Yeah, and in you too," he says, holding her swollen belly in his hands.

"*Ha!* You're sick." She laughs with a coy expression on her face.

"And you love me anyway," says Gabe, and then gently kisses her forehead.

Her face glows with warmth. "I do … we both do," she says as she presses her hands over his and looks down at her belly. "You know, I think I know when it happened."

"When I knocked you up?"

She rolls her eyes. "That too, but I mean when the change happened."

"Oh yeah? When was that?"

There's a knock on the door. An older Black man wearing a white coat and name tag that reads "Dr. Rhen" walks in.

"Mr. and Mrs. Mathis, how are you two today?" he asks.

"Doing fine, Doc" Gabe says.

"Hey, you're Moses' son, aren't you? How is he—" he stops himself. "Oh, I'm sorry. I forget that he's gone."

"It's all right. I do too sometimes." He looks away as he speaks.

"But," Chanel chimes in, "we're here for you to tell us about what's in our future today!"

"Yes, yes. Are you ready to find out about this baby?"

They look each other deeply in the eyes, and then turn their heads to face him with a smile.

Ashley A.T.

I

Six months earlier.

Late summers of southern Georgia have a heavy kind
of heat, an overwhelming hotness in the air that either
confines you inside, drawing you closer to those around you,
or tests you to see how long you can bear the elements,
trying not to let your blood boil from the outside in. It can
use your body and all of your judgments and senses to build
a bubbling rage that's ready to overflow and explode at any
moment. That's exactly why Theo, a young activist and dear
friend of Gabe and Chanel, picked this time of year to hold
his Peace Rally in the Park for the city of New Locale. He
wanted to give everyone, from both sides of the town, a
reason to come together for something good during these
trying times, and even added a back-to-school drive for the
kids, in hopes of teaching them early how to live with peace.
It's Saturday afternoon when Gabe and Chanel leave their

apartment, a safe enclosure of Love, and head for Central Park. Gabe drives down the old roads, gray and faded in color, as the sun beams fall through the tall oak trees with their millions of tiny green leaves, making lacy patterns on the street and gleaming down on his '02 Chevy coupe.

As he makes a right to turn onto West Main Street heading south, Gabe turns on the car radio and a woman's voice comes through the speakers.

"Hey everyone, you're listening to Infinite Radio, the sound of the city, where we're playing those timeless classics from yesterday, today, and tomorrow, and we'll keep playing them for all of Infinity, or as long as these airwaves keep carrying our message. I'm about to get out of this studio to go to Theo and Travis' Peace Rally in the park, so I'm leaving you with this new mixtape to fill your ears. I'll be back tomorrow. Peace, y'all. DJ MMS out."

The lofty piano of J. Cole's "Friday Night Lights (Intro)" begins. With his left hand on the steering wheel, Gabe leans on the armrest to his right, and reclines into his seat as he drives. His expression is cool. The sun is drawn to his calm demeanor and, like the car, its light reflects a streak of gold off his smooth dark skin. Though outwardly he is at ease as he maneuvers the car along the all-too-familiar roads, his eyes are alert, taking in every inch of his view, detailing it all in his mind, as his pupils scan the streets for anything out of the ordinary or unexpected. But the city is quiet today with everyone being at the rally, so any threat is at bay for now. Gabe recites the song's lyrics "… *It's funny how so close can seem so far, seem so far.*"

The next song, "Too Deep for the Intro", starts with a smooth, jazzy beat, and humming the chorus to herself in the passenger seat, Chanel smiles as she flicks her pink pen across a pink and white polka-dot planner, checking off her to-dos for her course assignments from the past week. She looks out the window and sighs happily. Something in the air feels different and it excites her.

"Oh, babe, isn't it great to be a part of something so… so *right*?" She beamed. "I think it's so nice the way Theo and Travis are so doing so much good for New Locale and the Church with this Peace Rally! Don't you feel good that we get to give back and help your hometown too?"

Gabe, nodding his head to the music, keeps his eyes on the road as he answers. "You know this is the last one of these we're going to, right?"

Her smile instantly falls she snaps her head in his direction.

Where Love Resides

"What are you talking about? Why would you say that?"

He smiles and answers calmly, "Cause we're leaving this bum ass town. Yeah, it's nice what Theo is doing and all, but things ain't changing out here."

Chanel sighs. Gabe is unbothered. Being born and raised in New Locale, he is tied to a bittersweet history with the city he grew up in. There isn't much to keep track of in this small town just off the southeast coast of Georgia, so he thinks he knows everything there is to know about it. He knows he feels comfortable on the West side, where his family and friends live, along with the recent addition of the New Locale University students. Folks on that side of town don't always have many resources or fancy possessions, but they have a sense of community that ties them together in their pursuits for something better. He knows the East side is full of uppity people—professors at the university, city officials in high positions, and their families—who are afraid of anything that looks different from them, like himself, so he stays away from there and the people if he can help it. Especially after his father was killed by a police officer on the East side, after he was leaving mistaken for the burglar he was chasing after from his job at the bank one night.

Shortly after, his mother decided to move for work, but Gabe and his brother stayed in the town they'd grown up in because they were comfortable here.

He always pays attention to his surroundings, being able to spot the slightest deviation from the norm around him, which is why he is a great fit as a campus security officer at the University. He recalled how one night, about a year or so after his father passed, Gabe saw a young woman studying late in the library. He reminds Chanel how his eyes lit up as her caramel skin and curly brown hair was illuminated, and her whole being seemed to glow under the fluorescent lights. He couldn't help but feel a pulling inside of himself, as if he was being drawn to her, but he left her alone, as he didn't want to interrupt her studying. It was past midnight as he was making his third lap around the floor, when he saw her nodding off at the table. Though he was locked in a trance as he gazed at her from afar, he was quick to see a male figure in the shadows who was approaching her from behind. Without thinking, Gabe rushed to her side, pinned the man to the bookcase, and saw that he was a young Westside local. They were known for targeting the students to loot their laptops and supplies.

Chanel woke up gently, unaware of the exchange that had taken place because of her presence, and turned to see the two of them behind her. As Gabe called for backup on his radio, she approached the thief, looked him firmly in his eyes, and asked "Are you okay? Why are you doing this?" Gabe watched her with his eyebrows raised in a puzzled expression, as the thief confessed he was trying to get money to buy his son a meal. Chanel had opened her bag, and pulled out a gift card that was in an envelope from her older sister, gave it to him, and asked Gabe to let the young man go. He had stared at her for a long time, and later told her, he should have dismissed her request and let the law handle him, but something made him stop and listen to her.

As the man ran off, she had told Gabe that her name was Chanel, and although he knew she wasn't from there, and he had thought if she was, she would for sure reside on the East side—the Southeast with the equally uppity people of color. Nonetheless, he knew that someone with a heart like hers needed to be protected. He thought that he should be the one to do the protecting and he knew that someday he would make her his wife. Chanel had heard this story a thousand times, and he wasn't wrong about any of it either. Gabe knew just about everything and everybody in New Locale, and now, after twenty-four years of living here, he has decided he's seen enough.

"Look, baby, once you finish this last semester we're out," he tells her. "I already been looking at security jobs in Atlanta. We can live a good life out there."

"I haven't agreed to any of this," she says, appalled at his lack of consideration for her opinions. "You know my final semester project is creating that community growth plan for New Locale. I've gotta see it through even after I graduate." She adds hopefully, "We all can make a difference here, don't you think?"

"No, I don't! I don't see how y'all have any hope for this place. You need to learn to look at things with a reasonable understanding grounded in the truth!" He slams his hands down on the steering wheel. "I've been here long enough to know how things are and how they're always going to—"

He turns to see Chanel's crestfallen face, as they drive through a patch of shadows, and realizes his pessimism seems to have touched her. The radio plays, "*Look, if this too deep for the intro I'll find another use, but just in case it's perfect let me introduce...*" He pulls to a stop sign.

"Well..." He leans closer to her, placing his hand on her leg. "Well, who knows? Maybe your plans will help. I've seen 'em, and you do have some really good ideas. I just know it'll take a lot of time and work for New Locale to get right, and you know my patience is running thin." She sits silently. "Okay, or maybe some old magic miracle spell coming out the sky will turn this place around overnight and we'll all be good, right?" he jokingly suggests, trying to lighten the mood. She isn't fazed by it. "And I was planning to talk to you about what happens next for us. We still have till your graduation to map it all out. I was just trying to think it out first. C'mon, Cha, don't do like this."

"Look," she starts with a solemn expression, "I know you have reason to feel the way you do about this place." She holds his hand where it rests on her leg. "I just… I want to believe things can change. You know a different New Locale than I do, because since I've been here I've seen so much good! They tell us all the time on campus that it's the twenty-somethings like us who create the future. You can't tell me you don't see just a *little* good around here lately?"

He turns to her. "Oh, I'm seeing something good right here in front of me," he says, sliding his hand to give her thigh a squeeze. "I been seeing the good here since the first time I saw your beautiful face in that library."

Her cheeks turn red as blush fills the caramel skin on her face, and she lets a slow smile form. "There was always good here. It's what led me to you, right?"

"Yeah, that part." With a cocky grin, he turns back to the road. The Erykah Badu sample from the song fades out: *"Ooh, hey, I'm trying to decide, which way to go, think I made a wrong turn back there somewhere..."* They're approaching the parking lot as they see the signs directing them towards the rally. Gabe parks, then he pauses for a moment, collecting himself.

"But for real, Cha, if it wasn't for you and my brother, I wouldn't still be here. I love that you can always see the good in things and people, but..." He stops, with his hand balled into a fist. "All I know is the hate that lives here. It's stronger than the little bit of good there is and I'm not trying to be here long enough to give that hate another chance to take anyone else from us."

She reaches out to gently hold his face.

"Baby, you're stubborn," she says with a tease, pulling the tiny coils of his beard. Her unexpected humor seems to take his mind away from his worries and ease his mood. "I don't know what it's going to take for you to see, but good is winning! The way we're doing things like going to this rally is making it happen right now. C'mon," she says as they get out of the car. "Let's enjoy the day before you start your shift. I'm not complaining!" she warns. "But I hardly see you since you're working nights again."

Where Love Resides

Gabe lifts a case of water from the car trunk while Chanel swings a bag of chips and various snacks to donate for the kids. They begin to walk down the sidewalk, heading toward the festivities. Apparently trying to remain unbothered by her remark, he slyly suggests, "You know, I could work daytime shifts in another city with some real jobs."

"So, you just want us to up and leave your brother here?"

"He'll be all right."

"Don't do Marcus like that! Why don't you apply for the New Locale police academy?"

Gabe's eyes widen, and she is taken aback as his nostrils flare. "Hell no! I ain't working for the crooked NLPD. They're half the problem in this town."

"What? How? I heard they're volunteering out here today. You know your skepticism is starting to sound irrational and crazy."

"Oh, word? Well let me rationally tell you that this is a crazy place with some crazy people, and we need to get out! Look." He nods in the direction of a young man dressed from head-to-toe in a blindingly bright white outfit, wearing a large T-shirt, jeans, and shoes, standing in the grassy area with his head down, fumbling with a cellphone. "There's Marcus. You can ask him too. What's good bro?" Gabe calls out as they approach him.

"Aye, *wassup*!" He smiles and extends his arms, hugging Chanel before he gives his brother a slap on the back. "Aye, y'all think my fit look fresh enough to post on the gram? I'm trying to find me a lil' rally baby out here today."

"*Ha*!" Gabe throws his head back. "Tell them they better put on some shades if they want to see you! But forget that. Man, please tell Cha how crooked NLPD is out here."

"Oh, girl, they all the way jacked up," Marcus says, throwing his hand in the air to show the levels of corruption he's witnessed. "They're so dirty I'd spit on one of them blue-badge bullies if they ever mess with me, and my own saliva would make them cleaner than they are!"

"See, he knows," Gabe says with a satisfied grin, glad he can count on someone to see things his way. "That's why I'm trying to tell her we have to get out."

Marcus freezes. "Whoa, man. What you mean leave? We New Locale soldiers, man. We got to stay here and do that we can to protect our people. The po-po sure ain't doing it. Who else you think will?"

Where Love Resides

Chanel cocks her head to the side, eyeing Gabe and waiting for his reply. He's expressionless for a moment, before he reluctantly concedes.

"Yeah, man, I feel you on that. I guess we'll see if there's anyone else thinking like y'all out here."

They approach the festivities in the center of the park. An arch made of balloons in red, blue, and yellow rises into the sky to welcome them. For all the hate that Gabe blames his city for, they sure don't see it out there. It looks as though everything good about New Locale and its residents have come together today. Piles and piles of donations cover the grass—backpacks filled with paper, pencils, and school supplies; stacks of chips, water, and a colorful assortment of snacks; and tons of little boys' and girls' toys to all be given away once school starts. Gabe and Chanel's are a mere drop in the sea of generosity before them.

Just past the donation area, children of all ages and races are laughing and playing as they run around the adults who stand in the grass, moving and grooving as the DJ plays summertime classics like Luther Vandross, Frankie Beverly & Maze, Tupac, and music that makes you forget your troubles and eases your soul. Not everyone is dancing though. In a white tent to the left, people dressed in fancy

17

fabrics sit in white folding chairs, peering out from behind big sunglasses or the corner of their eyes, watching the others like a spectacle.

"Eastside folks." Gabe points out, speeding up his pace to walk past before their eyes can cast judgment on them.

At the other end of all the activity, a small crowd of people have gathered in a circle to listen to a man speaking in a resonant voice. Gabe feels a hand grab his as Chanel leads him closer toward.

"We *must* continue to come together as one!" they hear the speaker say as the people clap. "The Good Lord's mission continues through *us*!"

"Tell it!" someone shouts.

"Now, go out into the world, letting the Spirit fill your hearts and guide you with Love for *all* whom you share this Earth with!"

"Amen," the crowd declares in unison, clapping as they began to disperse. Once they do, Gabe continues to follow behind Chanel and as she moves closer to the center, they see Reverend Anthony Brown with a great smile on his face, shaking hands with those who remain, telling them to "Be blessed" and thanking them for their time as they walk away.

"Rev!" Chanel calls out with enthusiasm. Gabe reaches to grab and keep her from alerting the reverend to their presence, but it's too late.

"Ahh, Sister *and* Brother Mathis! So nice to see the *both* of you today. How are you on this blessed Saturday?"

"Fine." Gabe retorts with a cold expression on his face. Chanel throws him a sharp glance.

"We're blessed to be a blessing, Rev," she replies. "We just caught the end of your speaking. You're always moving us to change through The Word and spread Love. I'm sorry we couldn't get here sooner!"

"Oh now, you didn't miss anything you haven't heard any other Sunday you're in service." He pauses. "Well, at least *one* of you didn't miss anything."

Gabe smiles a charmingly smug grin before he responds, "After I work all night down at the university, my amazing wife makes sure to fill me in on anything I did or *didn't* miss, Reverend."

"Gabe!" Chanel snaps.

Reverend Brown laughs lightly. "Your many hours of labor do not go unnoticed in His eyes, Brother Mathis. The Lord will continue to bless you for being a strong man and provider for Sister Mathis. Be thankful for her. In fact,

19

maybe you can thank Him for all your blessings first hand in service tomorrow, hm?"

"Yeah, maybe."

Chanel nudges her elbow into Gabe's side. "*We* will be there, Rev," she says.

"I look forward to seeing the two of you!" He drops his heavy hands on their shoulders, rocking them a bit with his firm grip and a smile. "Ah, now I've got to step away to handle some… church business, if you don't mind. Be blessed, Brother and Sister Mathis!"

Chanel immediately turns to Gabe as the reverend walks away. "What the hell is wrong with you?"

"Don't trust that man. These preachers ain't nothing but con men, selling *The Good Lord's Word*," he says, mimicking the reverend, "to people who need more than just a word to help them."

"Okay, and what's he doing by helping Theo and Travis with the Peace Rally?"

"Helping himself. Look." He points to the street just past the white tents, where they see a woman in a navy-blue pants suit step out of a limousine handing Reverend Brown a white envelope, which he slips into his pocket as he shakes her hand. Chanel frowns as Gabe uncertainty and

20

disappointment fill her mind, and winces an apology, feeling responsible for bringing her down, again.

"Cha, it's great that you want to be a part of something good. I wish more people had your hope and optimism, but we can't be out here blindly following anyone just because they put on a good show for the people. Look, he's about to get on that podium and give some more empty words to fill his pockets."

The music stops as Reverend Brown taps the microphone.

"Good afternoon, everyone!" He calls. "I hope you all are enjoying yourselves today, and I hate to interrupt, but I am pleased to inform you all that Mayor Banks has just let me know that because of our involvement with the annual Peace Rally and back-to-school drive, the St. Michael Baptist Church will be expanding its reach with a new community center at the Southeast end of the park, named after yours truly!"

"See what I mean?" Gabe tells Chanel. "Only thinking about his name. What about Theo? This was all his idea anyways."

Once the applause settles, Reverend Brown addresses the crowd again.

Ashley A.T.

"In addition to this, Mayor Banks also informed me that the Peace Rally will now be commissioned by the city, and she has decided to honor Theo Monroe and Travis Phillips with a Town Hero ceremony for all that they do for our community, not just today but every day. Let's have a few words from our heroes now!"

As everyone claps and cheers, Chanel looks at Gabe with a raised eyebrow. He doesn't look at her face, but feels her silently judging his skepticism, and begrudgingly claps as Travis is walking up to the stage.

"Thank you everyone! Thank you so much. This is a tremendous honor!" The young man says, waving his hands enthusiastically as he accepts the applause. "Truly, it's great to be rewarded for all the hard work I've put into this."

"Cha, now you can't tell me you don't feel some type of way about this. *Travis* is taking all the credit. Didn't even wait for Theo before eating up all the attention. He's another one fooling y'all, just looking out for himself."

She ignores him as she continues to clap, and Travis speaks.

"I know a lot of us Eastsiders don't always have the best reputation when it comes to our concern for *all* of New Locale. And these freckles and red hair on top of my pale skin don't help." He rubs the short buzzcut hair on his scalp

22

as the crowd responds with light laughter. "You know, I shout and scream about what we do, hoping you guys can see that I do care for all of us, and I thank you all for recognizing it, but I'd be lying if I said that I'm standing up here without the genuine heart and mind of my partner in crime, the ebony to the ivory of our dynamic duo, my best friend, Theo!"

The applause roars from the crowd, and Chanel claps hard enough to make up for Gabe's silence as he eats his prior words. Everyone cheers and looks for Theo to take the mic at the podium, but he doesn't appear.

"Theo, don't be shy today. C'mon up here!" Travis calls out.

Empty moments pass, and murmurs of worry and concern come from the half of the crowd where Gabe and Chanel stand, while *others* express laments of impatience and some even begin to leave. The enthusiasm Travis showed turns to nervous anxiety, and Gabe studies his expression from afar, thinking to himself to avoid Chanel's judgment, *The guy talks a good game, but his actions... First, he jumps to the stage, and now he doesn't have the slightest clue where Theo is.*

Ashley A.T.

Someone shouts, "Hey, here he comes!" and a collective sigh of relief fills the air as everyone looks to the right. The sun is setting in the west, and soft orange clouds fill the pink and blue sky, casting a brilliant glow over a brigade of laughing, smiling children who tug and push a coy Theo through the crowd to the podium. As he makes his way to the front, the people share cheers, patting him on the back, giving individual expressions of thanks as he humbly accepts their love and gratitude. Even Gabe sports an exuberant smile, seeing his friend rightfully honored, finally. As Theo reaches the stage, Travis stands behind him and lifts Theo's arms in the air, getting him to take in his rightful due from the people who admire, support, and love him.

Theo addresses the people in his soft-spoken and sincere voice. "Oh, wow! Thank you all so much. You have no idea how happy it makes me to see everyone here today, to see that you all care about each other so much, seeing your generosity in gifts and taking the time to help shape our future. To hear that this rally has support from those at the highest levels of New Locale to even the everyday person like you and me." He pauses and pushes his glasses back in place. "Um, you know, it's definitely an honor to be recognized as a 'hero'," he continues with an unsettling look in his bright brown eyes, "but I'm going to have to reject the mayor's invitation."

A collective gasp comes from the crowd, and all eyes and ears wait for an explanation.

"I'm rejecting it because no one should be considered a hero for doing what we all are capable of and should be doing for our community every day. I'm happy to set an example for the kids coming up here, but just last week we lost an innocent Black man's life to the carelessness of a cop, and no one aside from his friends and family did anything to show that Henry Davis' life mattered. I myself witnessed so many people watch the story on the news, giving it just a moment of their attention before returning to their regular daily lives, like it was a weather report."

Everyone is silenced by their own guilt as they listen, thinking about their actions, reflecting on their lack of doing and minimally passive concerns after hearing the news.

"This happens far too often for us to continue to not take action and do something to protect our friends, family, neighbors, and anyone else we share this community with. Henry was just as important to this city as any else of us here right now, and I wouldn't want to see any of you lose your life in the untimely or unjust manner that he did.

Ashley A.T.

"Some of you know that I do a segment on the university's radio station called New Locale Matters, where I talk about issues that are important here because I care so much about who resides in this city, but it seems that some of us don't matter, and until we all do, I've decided to renounce my name and instead would like to be referred to as 'Hashtag It Don't Matter'. It doesn't matter what I do, because as a Black man this city, and in this nation, my name does not matter any more than our lives do. Thank you all for coming today. I hope I haven't spoiled the mood." Theo steps back from the podium and stands solemnly behind his words that are still settling in the minds of the listeners, who are silent as they digest them.

Marcus breaks the silence of the moment, shouting passionately, "I don't know about y'all, but Theo matters to me! 'Hashtag He Matters'!"

People begin to clap in agreement with his sentiments, and Travis jumps back to the podium at the chance to build on their passions.

"That's right," he says, pounding his fist on the wooden surface, "Theo matters! Let them know. Hashtag He Matters! Hashtag He Matters! Hashtag He Matters!"

As he chants, the people begin to chant along with him, raising their voices as one so everyone in and around

26

the park can feel their love for him. All but Theo are in unison, and soon he takes his place back at the microphone.

"Please, everyone!" he pleads. "Thank you, I really appreciate your love, but this isn't the point I'm trying to make. If my voice can't be used for everyone then—"

A piercing screech from the speakers cuts off his speech, and as everyone cringes, covering their ears from the disturbing sound, they look to see a police officer holding the cords from the microphone in his hands with a menacing look on his face.

"Attention everyone!" he yells, with no need for a mic as the hate amplifies his voice. "We've received noise complaints from the residents in the area and are kindly asking you all to go home, *now*!"

Theo begins to step down from the podium, shaking his head at the irony of his voice being silenced so unrightfully as he was trying to make his point.

"Officer," he starts, "I'm sorry about any noise, but—"

The officer snatches the aviator shades off his face before he speaks. "Hey, *boy*, did I stutter? This unauthorized protest is over! Y'all wrap this up before we have to start making arrests."

Gabe clenches his fist and Chanel grabs his arm while releasing a horrified gasp as they watch the ordeal. Everyone is still buzzing from their passionate displays to support Theo, and having it so hatefully threatened, they turn their energy of Love into something resembling Hate and direct it at the police officer, who himself now clearly feels threatened by their piercing. Travis, unafraid and upset, hurries toward the officer.

"Unauthorized?" he asks. "What do you mean, unauthorized? The mayor herself has endorsed this *peaceful rally,* not protest!" Red in the face, he thrusts an angry finger just inches away from the officer's face. "How dare you barge over here, telling us we can't be here! Who gave you permission to do such a thing, *sir*?"

Asserting his power, the officer grabs Travis by the shirt collar, pulling the young man up to his face so they are eye to eye. "I don't know what you're trying to prove out here for..." He looks around. "But you will address *me* as Officer Bailey! You got that?" He pushes Travis away, nearly knocking him to the ground as he stumbles back. "This park is in *my* jurisdiction, and I did not sign off on some raucous *rally* that's disturbing *my* residents who called in from the East side of the park. And now that I'm here I can clearly see these speaker wires are not up to code, there are too many… people loitering on the grounds, and I could write you up for the piles and piles of trash dumped in the front of the area!"

Marcus pushes his way to the front. "The only trash here is dressed in that dusty blue uniform!"

Everyone laughs, but Gabe swiftly pushes Chanel behind him, and rushes to his brother's side, herding him out of Bailey's line of sight. The mocking laughter only intensifies the officer's defensive state, and as his face turns red and beads of sweat began to drip from his head, he places his right hand on the holster on his hip. Catching Bailey's movement, Reverend Brown quickly steps up, bearing a warm smile to put the man at ease.

"Now, Officer Bailey, sir, I think this is all just one big misunderstanding. As a man of the Lord, I can attest that these young men have done a fine job of ensuring that all of their T's were crossed and I's were dotted when coordinating this good-hearted event! I can respect a man of the law, doing his job to protect the grounds he serves." He turns so he's speaking to both Bailey and the crowd now. "It is our calling to be a *loving* servant for Him, isn't it?"

"Amen!" someone calls out.

"That's all the good Officer Bailey was doing here today, right? Can we find it in our hearts to show just a little appreciation for this dutifully righteous man?" The reverend faces the crowd wholly now so the officer can't see his expression—a big grin and raised eyebrows, clearly pleading for agreement in this moment. It's understood by all, and they clap and express small gestures of gratitude, most of which come from the folks under the white tent.

"Oh, well, thank you all. That's very kind," Bailey replies, as the tension in his face dissipates—though he keeps a hand close to his hip. "I just need to ensure that this is all in regulation for you to continue whatever you have going on. Things can get out of hand pretty quickly over here, and that pile of junk is just asking to attract all kinds of looters and danger."

"We do apologize if our celebration disturbed the residents around here," Reverend Brown continues. "And it'll be sundown before you know it. There's plenty of room in the church basement to store the generous amount of *donations* we received today! Would some of these fine young men be able to help take them down?" He gestures towards the church.

"I gotcha, Rev!" Travis volunteers.

Where Love Resides

"Me and Marcus are on it too," Gabe asserts, before shooting a leery glance at Travis. The three of them walk off, and a few other men join them.

"That's great," says Bailey. "But, unless I see some type of paperwork with the permits for the event, I will have to issue a citation to the organizer." He looks at Theo. "Can you provide that, bo—, excuse me, young man?"

"Not exactly," Theo says softly, with a tense expression. "I'm not sure where the paper—"

"Theo! I have it right here," Chanel calls out, pulling a folder of papers out of the planner in her purse. "Remember you asked me to make copies on campus the other day?"

Theo's face floods with a bright glow of relief. "You're a lifesaver, Cha!"

"All right, if you two can follow me to my cruiser so I can look up the permit number in the system, we can all be on our way," says Bailey.

"Thank *God* all is well!" The reverend beams with arms outstretched toward the heavens. "Everyone else, please feel free to enjoy yourselves. We have the park grounds till ten o'clock according to the permit. There's still

31

enough time to eat, be merry, and bask in the glow of Love on this beautiful evening."

The DJ puts on music, bringing back the good vibes from earlier, and everything is as it was before. Chanel and Theo are back in no time after Officer Bailey confirmed that they had every right and permission to be out there. Gabe and Marcus are still in the church with Travis. The men had formed an assembly line from the park to the rear of the church, passing boxes and bags along from one man to the next, until they reached the storage closet where the line ended with Gabe, Marcus, and Travis.

"So, Travis," Gabe starts, "you really put on a good selfless act out there. What's that about?"

Stacking the boxes with a smile, Travis says, "It's not an act! We're all one people, brother. I'm just trying to do my part to look out for us all."

"One people?" Gabe drops the bag of clothes in his hands and stands across from him. "Nah, we're living very different lives on this side of town. Why are you over here anyways? Why not stick to helping the eastside while we hold it down over here?"

Without missing a beat as he continues arranging the items Travis replies, "Those eastside kids have more than enough to do well over there. The mayor is making sure all the city funds stay on that side too." He shakes his head. "I just want to help Theo do what we can to help everybody. He's quiet, but moves the people with his passionate pleas. I'm loud and can get all in City Hall's face to complain about what's wrong without them turning me away. We all have a part we can play in making things right."

Gabe is silent as Marcus says, "Man, stop trying to check Travis. He been down since the days on the playground with me and Theo. It's the bullies like Bailey we need to be watching out for. You saw how he jacked up this man earlier," he says smoothing out Travis's shirt. "Can't trust the cops to protect anyone."

Gabe's eyes widen as he gasps, "Chanel!"

"Go check on her," Travis advises. "We've got the rest down here."

Giving him one final look over, Gabe says, "All right. C'mon, Marcus."

The two of them make their way back to rejoin the others after ensuring that Travis was indeed handling things in a trustworthy manner.

Gabe grabs Chanel's hand and gives it a squeeze as he calls out, "Yo, Theo, we're 'bout to get out of here—I'll be starting my shift soon. But you really did your thing out here

33

today. New Locale got some work to do, but you might actually set this city straight." They clasp hands, and he gives Theo a strong pat on the back.

"Hey, man, thank you," Theo replies humbly. "You're right about the work, but it'll be you that makes the difference, not me."

"*Ha!* Yeah, all right. And one day Marcus will finally impress one of the girls he harasses too, huh?"

"You tell me," Theo says pointing afar to Marcus, who is romancing a young lady.

"So, you like how I asserted my opinion earlier?" Marcus is asking her. "I couldn't just let my boy Theo walk out here thinking he don't matter to us, and I damn sure wasn't about to let no police disrespect him. I'm trying to see how I can respect you though, girl."

They all laugh as Marcus turns to give them a thumbs up with a big smile on his face as he leads the woman away.

"He's right though, Gabe," Chanel chimes in. "You've started something good, Theo, and we'll do our part to keep it up. I gotta show you what I have planned for my senior project. I'll definitely need your input on it."

Theo's eyes light up. "Yes! We all have to be in this. That makes me happy, Cha. Really, thank you so much."

Where Love Resides

Chanel gives him a warm hug, and then she and Gabe make their way toward their car. It's dark now, and they walk close together as they approach the still oak trees that line the sidewalk. An eerie feeling grows on Chanel's skin as she leans in and peers into the dark shadows between the trees. Looking deeper beside one particular tree, she gasps and grabs Gabe's arm when she sees a face gazing back at her.

"Who's there?" Gabe asks, standing protectively in front of Chanel.

"Oh, I didn't mean to frighten you," says a soft, weary voice as an older woman steps into the moonlight. Her copper-skinned face bears so many deep wrinkles, she looks as if she stepped out of the tree bark, rather than the shadows next to it.

"Mrs. Yamassee," Chanel says with a sigh of relief. "What are you doing there?"

"*Nah kuh chah kih*," she says in her native tongue. "This is sacred land we stand on. Powerful energies surround us." Her long black hair that falls to her waist gently blows in the wind. "Just taking it in while I can."

Ashley A.T.

Goosebumps rise on Chanel's arm as the breeze touches her skin. She smiles at Mrs. Yamassee's elderly wisdom, while Gabe stares at her with a blank expression.

"Can we give you a ride somewhere?" he asks.

"Oh, no. Thank you," she replies. "The other Seven Corners girls should be swinging by to take me home soon. You all get home safe. I'll be seeing you around."

She turns and fades back into the shadows between the trees, and although they don't see the car, they hear it arrive and pull off into the night.

"You know she's a witch, right?" Gabe says.

"All right, that's enough of your crazy talk."

"I'm serious!" he says. "Check this out. They named the Seven Corners convenience store after her and her friends because they are from all seven of the continents. Mrs. Y is Native American, right? Ms. Bajomo is from Nigeria, Mrs. Chen is Chinese, and I can't tell you the rest of them because I haven't met them all. In fact, no one has ever seen all seven of them at the same time, because..." He leans in and lowers his voice. "They're all the same person. One witch, one spirit with different bodies."

"Wow, wow, wow!" says Chanel, throwing her head back in a roaring laugh. "So you really are crazy? Who knew I was in love with a lunatic?"

36

"Hey, you don't have to believe me! But—" He pulls her close and presses her body against his. "Did I just hear you say you're in love with me? Even after a whole year together?"

"With your crazy flaws and all," she says as they kiss underneath the stars. "Too bad you have to go to work tonight."

"Oh, I was lying so we could leave. You got me all to yourself tonight, girl."

"*What*?" She yelps excitedly as her eyes light up. "You know I *hate* having to sleep without you. Let's go!"

Gabe stops to watch Chanel jump into the car, amazed at how someone like her can love a person like him so perfectly with all of his imperfections, and in that moment, he can't think of a single flaw in her.

Damn, I'm lucky, he thinks. *Too bad it ain't more love in the world. Wouldn't it be something if we all felt like this?*

He gets in the car with her, and they drive home to their apartment, wrapped up in the essence of Love.

II

By midnight, all is quiet in New Locale. Only a handful of cars remain on the road as the drivers make their way to their final destination for the evening. Lights are out in the small shops and local businesses' windows are shuttered. The small town seems to be holding its breath, hushed by a "calm before the storm" feeling in the air.

In the park behind the church, Travis and Theo and Travis are packing away the last of the donations and setup from the rally.

"Aye, Theo, you got anyone who can donate some massage chairs to the church? You killed 'em today with all the support the city showed, but now my back is killing me." Travis groans as he stretches.

"That pain should feel good, knowing it's about to make a big difference out here! At least I hope it does," Theo says in his soft yet distinguished voice. Peering out from his black hoodie, he gazes contemplatively at the City Hall off in the distance.

"Are you kidding? I'm telling you, my back is feeling all the impact you're making out here." Travis shakes his head. "I'm the one wondering if being the loud-mouth White boy from the East side coming to the West is really making any difference. You could do this all on your own to be honest, man."

Theo breaks his gaze with a sharp turn of the neck. "*Pshh!* Get out of here," he says, tossing his hand in the direction of his friend. "We're a team. We're showing everyone it's possible to do right by each other. If you're winning, then I'm winning, and we're making the town better by winning together. No one would pay attention to this young Black man that don't matter in the world if I didn't have my loud-mouth White brother from another beside me." Theo slaps Travis's back in a joking manner.

"*Ow!*" Travis whines, as he lets the case of water he is carrying fall to the ground, causing one of the plastic bottles to burst with an explosive *POW!* that echoes loudly into the distance.

"Ooh, my bad, bro." The two stare down at the water spilling out on the ground, like two children waiting to see if

39

there will be any consequences for an innocent mistake. After a few moments, suspecting that no harm has been done, Travis says, "It's cool, man. You know what? I'm going to get that toy wagon I saw in the church basement for the rest of this, since you want to play around."

"Ooh!" Theo snaps his fingers, triggered by a sudden thought. "There's some speakers in the basement too. Can you set them up out here tomorrow? I recorded my episode for the *NL-Matters* show and want to use the them to broadcast it out here. I really want this one to be heard. Something told me we need it."

Furrowing up his red eyebrows, Travis studies Theo closely. "Yeah, but why are you asking me like you won't be here or something?"

"Huh? Oh… yeah. I don't know why I— never mind. Just help me set it up then, all right?"

"I got you. Now back to the matter of these water bottles. I'm going to get that wagon." Travis starts to turn towards the church.

Theo grabs his shoulder. "Hey, I just wanted to say…" He pauses to gather his thoughts. "Thanks for always being by my side, man. Like, from the time we were kids, you always had my back, and even when I'm not sure about things, you come with your own way of looking at things, your optimism that always keeps me motivated. New Locale needs your voice to help everyone, just as much as it's helped me."

Theo reaches out his other hand, and Travis's confusion slowly dissolves into a moment of acceptance, somehow feeling the magnitude of this moment.

Their two hands clasped together, he replies with a smile, "Through thick and thin, my brother. I don't know where all of this is coming from, but you know we got each other till we six deep. And even then I'll come looking for you on the other side!"

"*Haha*, true that, man! True that. But anyways, I'll be out here breaking down the rest of the setup. If Rev is there, can you tell him to come out? I want to ask him about getting the message around to everyone tomorrow."

"For sure!" Travis starts to walk off. "And remember, the world will know you matter one day! 'Hashtag He Matters'!"

"At least I know one person thinks so!" Theo smiles as he starts to disassemble a table on the grass.

Ashley A.T.

Officer Brandon Bailey slows his car to a crawl as he approaches Central Park and uses his sternest voice to call into the New Locale Police Department dispatch.

"Breaker-breaker, this is Officer Bailey, cruising southbound on East Park Avenue, responding to reports of an unidentified disturbance in the park. Some kind of explosion. Likely gunshots."

A woman on dispatch responds, "Ten-four, Officer. Any other details you can observe from your current position?"

"I'm seeing a suspicious figure on the southwest end of the park. I'm pulling in to investigate. Stand by." He stops the car along the street, hidden in the darkness by the tall oak trees lining the sidewalk.

"We're sending backup to your location now. Is there an immediate threat of danger?"

"I don't need backup, Janet," he snaps back. "This is my territory; I'll handle any situation taking place!"

"Sir," she starts. "You would be in violation of your citation in moving on the ground alone. After your last incident, we can't allow you—"

"Ten-four," he interrupts. "Standing by." He quickly flips the switch, turning off the radio. Grimacing at the figure standing in the grass, he lets out an impatient sigh.

Where Love Resides

They want me to sit back and watch another West-side boy bring down our town with more crime? He thinks to himself. *And so, what about 'my last incident.' I was doing my duty to protect this park from them."*

He looks at the picture sitting up on his dashboard, of a young child with curly brown hair, smiling in his elementary school uniform, and says aloud, "Don't worry, Daddy's keeping his promise to keep this place safe for you... Always."

The figure in the park is now kneeling on the ground. Bailey squints his eyes, tightening his grip on the steering wheel with red knuckles bulging as he becomes more impatient.

"What is he doing? And where the hell is that backup?"

The figure in the park stands up, and Officer Bailey sees what appears to be a long black object in his hands.

"It's a gun!"

His mind is on autopilot as he jumps out of his vehicle, leaving the car door open. The moment his heavy boots hit the ground he starts running toward the figure at top speed, his hand already on his gun.

Theo collapses the last banner on the grass, puts it in the carrying case, and is just standing up, smiling as he prepares to head back inside, when he sees a man, a police officer, burst out of the dark running in his direction.

"Don't freaking move!" the officer yells across the park, pulling his gun out of its holster and aiming it right at him.

He freezes in place and feels the color drain from his frightened face. He slowly assumes the position, lifting his hands in the air, trembling as he begins to recite The Lord's Prayer. "Our Father in heaven, hallowed be thy name…"

"Shut up!" The officer stops about twenty feet away with his feet spread apart and the hair on his arms sticking straight up, he holds the gun out in front of him. In the dim glow of the street light, Theo can see beads of sweat rolling down the man's red face, his eyes locked on Theo with an intense, fevered stare. He recognizes the officer: Bailey, from the rally. Theo continues reciting the last verses of the prayer. He can barely hear himself, let alone the officer over the pounding of his heart, numbing his senses as the blood fiercely pumps through his veins.

His shaking causes the banner to start to slide out of its zipper case, and as he instinctively reaches to catch it,

Officer Bailey's eyes widen in fear at the sudden movement. As he tightens the grip on his gun, the sound of the bullet leaving the barrel resounds throughout the park.

* * *

"*Noooooo!!!!!*" Travis cries out from the sidewalk, as he watches his friend's last moments of life before Theo's dead body collapses to the ground.

Two policemen Travis has met before: Officer Creek, a twenty-something-year-old Seminole, and Officer Sanders, a young White cop in his early thirties, come running up behind Bailey, who is still holding the gun in place. They stop in their tracks when they see Theo's body lying on the ground too.

Bailey seems to come back to his senses and faces the men.

"Officers, it's about time you showed up! Let's get an ID on this kid, and—"

"That's Theophilus Monroe, sir," Officer Creek interrupts somberly. "Most recently known as 'Hashtag It Don't Matter'. Remember, he did Peace Rally today?"

Ashley A.T.

Travis just about reaches his friend with Reverend Brown following him, and Officer Bailey tells his men, "Get the body. Hurry up, quick!"

"Don't touch him!" Travis yells as he dives onto the grass, reaching out for Theo, just as Officer Sanders does the same. They both slide along the ground for a second, and the moment when their hands should have landed on Theo, they're both instantly repelled back, thrown onto their rear for a few feet, by some force that surrounds the body.

Reverend Brown slows his jog as he catches up to where Travis is lying on the ground, at the same time Bailey and Creek are picking up their comrade, brushing the dirt off his uniform. Travis is pushing himself up, when he feels a deep shaking pulse coming up from the ground, trembling through his hands and knees.

Creek flinches and jumps, freezing with his hands out in fear of the unknown disturbance. "W-what is that?"

Suddenly two waves of light shoot out of the grass from each side of Theo's body and ascend into the sky, resembling a thin, watery wall-like barrier that confines the officers to the East side of the park and Reverend Brown and Travis to the West side. Everyone gasps as they marvel in fear and confusion at the supernatural event taking place.

Where Love Resides

"The curse…" Reverend Brown exclaims, gazing up into the heavens, where the barriers seem to have no end.

Creek points to the north side of the city to his right. "Look, they go out past the station. It looks like they're cutting right through the middle of City Hall!"

They all then turn to the south. The barrier extends as far as the eye can see in that direction as well, not damaging any of the buildings, cars, or trees in its path, but floating right through them. All the men now face each other. The younger faces of Travis and the other officers bearing expressions of bewilderment and confusion, while Reverend Brown and Officer Bailey know exactly what is happening, again.

Before anyone can gather their composure, Theo's body then begins to rise off of the ground. Their heads all instantly turn downward and slowly lift as they watch him levitate into the air, leaving only a pool of blood and the case with the banner underneath him.

Without saying a word, Travis scrambles to pull his cellphone out of his pocket. He presses a few buttons on the screen, turning on the camera so he can record what is happening.

"Hey, stop that!" yells Officer Sanders.

Travis pays him no attention as he continues recording.

"What are you doing? Make him stop!" Bailey commands as he smacks the man on his shoulder pushing him forward.

Sanders takes a few steps and attempts to grab the phone through the barrier, but as soon as his arm crosses through, he freezes, and his body begins to tremble violently. Travis quickly turns his camera away from Theo, now some hundred feet in the air, and aims it at the officer caught in the barrier's current.

"Jim!" Creek yells and is about to run toward him, but Bailey holds his arm in front to stop him, just as the barrier flows into Officer Sanders and turns bloody red as it engulfs and swallows him until he disappears.

"Oh my god! What is happening?" cries Creek, wide-eyed and holding his head in his hands, trying to make sense of what has just taken place. Bailey turns around and pulls out a cellphone of one of his pockets.

"Yeah, it's me. Wake up the mayor and—I know what time it is! Get her up! And have someone look up the friend of that Theo-don't-matter boy… Yeah, the White one. I'll explain once I'm there but get her up *now*! Yeah … bye."

He grabs Creek, who is still distraught and mumbling unintelligibly.

"Let's go. You're riding in my car."

"Okay!" he replies, still stunned to near numbness, as he follows Bailey across the grass, through shadows between the trees, and into his car as it speeds off in the direction of City Hall.

"Rev, we have to get Theo," Travis shouts. "He's still low enough for, I don't know, a fire truck or a ladder, to reach him? No, a helicopter! I'm calling the police."

The reverend regards him, with sympathy and replies, "Boy, did you not just see what *the police* did to him?"

"Yeah, but not all cops are bad, right? There's got to be someone who can help save him."

"Son, look up." The reverend points in the air. As Travis followed the motion of his hand, he watches Theo's body ascend higher and higher into the sky, until he passes the night clouds and is out of their sight. "He's out of our hands now. We have to let go and let God handle this."

"No! We have to do *something* for him," Travis cries with a shaky voice, as the realization that his friend is gone starts to settle into his heart and mind. He looks around frantically, pondering possibilities and pointless options. "Something? Anything…?"

Reverend Brown watches as grief and desperation overcome this young man, who was fighting within himself to avoid the acceptance of this reality. Although he'd seen death come like a thief in the night many times before, at the hands of many others like Officer Bailey, robbing countless friends and families alike of the lives to be shared with their loved ones, and although he'd always known exactly what to say to console their sadness, known what to do to ease their spirit, this time, he finds that the distress pouring out of Travis's face has lodged itself inside him too, and he struggles himself to let Death numb him into acceptance.

This time he let the struggle move him, as he takes a few steps in Travis's direction; and he lets his heart lead him as he wraps his arms around the young man, muffling his sobs and looking East through the strange barrier. "We'll make sure they know Theo mattered" he assures him. "That's all we can do now to break the Curse of the Red Sea."

"The what—" Travis starts to ask, but stops as he looks down at the pool of blood that had spilled into the earth, like the water from the bottle that fell, and instantly he feels the guilt and remorse settle like a rock in his throat, silencing him for the rest of the night.

Ashley A.T.

III

The stars of the night, shining like specks of glitter in the distance, fade away as the sun's morning glow arrives, illuminating the sky with a soft orange light that creeps through the curtains and Gabe catches it glisten across Chanel's skin as they wake up. It's Sunday. Her eyes slowly open and he sees the look of confusion on her face, the same state he's found himself in too. Feeling something different in the air, he's lost in the moments of transitioning out of a dream and into the day's awaiting reality. Nothing seems wrong or out of the ordinary to him, yet, as he comes to his senses. His eyes adjust, making out the familiar shapes of their surroundings, seeing the tan wooden nightstand next to them and recognizing the gold clock reading 9:35 AM. He recognizes the two glasses of water, one half empty, and the one to the left of it, half full and smudged lipstick on the rim. Before he realizes why the second one makes him smile, the white curtains fluttering in front of the open window let a gentle autumn breeze flow in, nudging Chanel to roll over. The metal bed frame creaks as she turns and reveals a pair of bright brown eyes that instantly lock with his.

"Good morning, love," Gabe's soft, deep voice murmurs.

It's his goal to somehow, before her mind can process the day or time, or think about any troubles that found the city the previous night, to fill her ears and her heart with all of the tenderness they can hold this morning, and every other morning that's mattered since they were married.

She extends her hand to hold his face and asks, "Wait, this is real right? This isn't still some unreal fantasy that escaped my dreams?"

She softly strokes his all too real face and allows her fingers to play in the coarse hairs of his low beard. He pulls her close to him, and she raises an eyebrow with surprise as his strong hands hold her bare back.

"Can you have the nights off more often, please? I need more mornings like this in my life. And," she says, biting her lip and gazing at his, "nights like that too." Her eyes make their way up and down his chiseled brown body.

"There's that face again," he admires the glow she radiates with confidence in seeing the effect he still has on her, even after a year of mostly blissful matrimony. He pulls her even closer, pressing her body against his, embracing her curves and using his fingers to stroke her soft caramel skin.

"I might not have another night off for a while, but we've got this morning, we have right now," he says. His cocky grin exposes a Colgate smile that lights up her eyes.

"Wait," she says, gently pushing away. "It's Sunday, isn't it? What time is it? We'll be late for service!"

Gabe's smile instantly dissolves as he kisses his teeth and rolls his eyes. "Mood killer," he grumbles. "Can't we miss one little Sunday service? We were just at the church for the Peace Rally yesterday."

She cuts her eyes and glares at him for a moment. "You're just a heathen looking for an excuse to sin early this Sunday morning, huh?" she asks as her mouth draws into a playful smile.

His eyes light up. "Yes! I'm a sinner. Come here and give me something to repent for," he says as he grabs her, tossing the duvet over both of them. Playful laughs and screams fill the room as they indulge and explore each other's mind, body, and soul.

Where Love Resides

While the two of them find and make their way to
Love, their phones on the dresser both glow with texts and
alerts carrying the morning news. But, just as they were
when the tragedy took place, once again they're caught up in
the bliss they find in each other, and in the safety their love
as they face the day, transitioning from their Lovers' Dream
and into a tragic reality.

Afterwards in their tiny apartment, steam escapes
from under the bathroom door as Chanel is finishing up her
shower, and the vapors meets Gabe in the kitchen. He
inattentively listens to New Locale's Sunday Morning news
on the TV in the living room as he pours himself a cup of
coffee. He turns to reach for the old wooden cabinet, no need
to take a step or stretch his arm too far in the small space to
open it, and scans the shelves for the creamer.

He leans over to the short hall where the bathroom is
and asks, "Cha, did you move the coffee creamer?"

"I put it on the counter—where you always drink your
coffee," she responds.

He turns his head and sees it waiting right in front of
him. As he starts to grab it, his hand bumps a green vase

55

holding wilting roses, the ones he bought Chanel for their anniversary the week before.

"Love you, babe," he yells.

"You better!" she calls back.

As he stirs in the creamer, he gazes at the roses, with their brown withered edges, and begins to think about what's next for the two of them. Love was more than picking up some drugstore flowers that would sit in a vase and die, every year, till he passed, or she did, or even worse, if their love died before them. He wants to give her more. For all the ways she shows she loves him, she deserves a garden of roses, or some way for their love to carry on forever.

Something the news reporter says catches Gabe's attention. A woman with an Afro addresses the camera.

"The developing story of the day is the 'Return of the Curse of the Red Sea'. We've been trying to gather details from local witnesses and police reports about an incident that took place just after midnight last night in Central Park, where a young man was shot and killed by a police officer."

"Cha, you hear this?"

Chanel steps out of the bathroom, wrapped in her towel and stands beside him as the anchorwoman continues.

"Reports and complaints from around the town are coming in, with many saying that the barrier from the curse

56

has prevented them from getting where they have to go this morning. As those who were here last time recall, anyone without a pure intent in their heart will not be able to cross through. Our own Ron Howard is on the scene in Central Park where the incident took place. We'll go to him live now. Ron, tell us what's going on."

A tall handsome man brushes the hair out of his face before he speaks. Looking into the camera he says, "Thank you, Robin. I'm here on the East side of Central park this morning, where you can faintly see the barrier that's causing so much disruption this morning. No one has been able to, or even tried to, cross through it, as many are being forewarned by elders around the city who tell legends and superstitions of this 'Red Sea' curse that came over New Locale before." He puts his hand over his mouth to try to hide the mocking smirk on his face. "I'm here with Mrs. Josephine Taylor, who says she called the police last night after hearing a loud noise in the park before the shooting occurred. Now Mrs. Baker, can you tell us exactly what you heard and saw?"

The old woman standing beside him fixed her glasses as she speaks to him. "Why, yes," she starts "I was just winding down for the day. I'd just gone upstairs and given my husband Todd his glass of seltzer water to put his teeth in, because it's just fowl when he leaves them out on the nightstand, smelling up the room with the stench of tuna salad he eats before bed. But never mind that. So I was upstairs when I heard this *POP!* come from the park. I didn't want to bother going back downstairs to investigate, so I called the police naturally." She shrugs. "It was quiet after that, so I thought everything was fine. But just when I was getting ready to lie down, I heard more noise! This time it sounded like a gunshot for sure. So I got up to look out the window and out of nowhere this blinding light came through the window! I could see it over the trees and I knew it was the curse come back again. I remember the first time it happened when they lynched the little negro—*oh!* I mean, the little boy."

"Thank you Mrs. Taylor," he says leading the camera away from the woman.

Chanel looks at Gabe. "Were you here when it happened before?"

"No, that was way back. In the sixties, I think. My pops told me about it one time before…" he trails off. "I'll break it down for you later," Gabe says.

Walking along the sidewalk, with the barrier still behind them, Ron continues the report. "Police are lined up along the East side of the park where the incident happened and doing their best to advise residents to keep a distance, but as you can see the barrier runs straight up and down the center of the city, so the department can't survey the entire length. We are also advising you to take caution not to attempt to cross, in case whatever mythological phenomenon or whatever occurs," he says, unable to contain the laugh he lets out.

Just then two kids in the background run across the grass heading right towards the center of the park. The camera man's finger is seen as he points to silently alert Ron, still laughing. When he finally does pay attention and turns around to shout "Hey, stop!" The kids reach the center of the park, running and giggling as they pass through unscathed at all.

Ron stops for a moment, gazing at them as they reach the West side of the park and run out of sight. Then he turns to the camera, "Well there you have it folks! Our first stab at debunking this rumored 'Red Curse'. Let's go in for a closer look now that we can all clearly see nothing is going to happen."

The camera bounces as they hurry over to the center.

"Viewer discretion is advised here, folks. It appears that the blood from the unnamed suspect—or victim, still looks fresh, as if it hasn't dried since the incident took place. I'm going to pick up this black case lying here to see what's inside now, and—"

As he reaches his arm inside, his body jolts to a stop, and the waters engulf him, just like the officer the night before. Chanel's hands cover her mouth as she gasps, and Gabe's coffee cup slips out of his hand and shatters on the countertop.

"Ron!" The camera man shouts. All that's seen are his feet running on the grass as he drops the camera to the ground. The screens returns to Robin, sitting at her desk, wide-eyed before she quickly gathers her composure.

"Um, well," she starts in a fluster, "As Ron said before, no names have been released as far as the suspect or the police officer, but Mayor Banks is preparing to address the situation from the steps of City Hall later this morning. We'll continue updating you on this story, and asking you all to send Ron Howard and his family well wishes at this time, along with anyone else who may be affected by this strange phenomena in the coming hours. Sadly, this news comes just one day after New Locale's own Theo Monroe's, a.k.a. 'Hashtag It Don't Matter', annual Peace Rally, in the same park where the incident took place. We haven't been able to get a word from him or his manager Travis Philips this morning—"

"Manager?" Gabe repeats. "Since when is he his—"

"*Shhh!*" Chanel quiets him.

"—but I'm sure we'll hear some words of hope and healing from his 'New Locale Matters' segment tonight at 8:30 PM. Until then we'll continue updating you on this story. This is Robin Reed for New Locale News in the Morning. Please be safe, everyone."

Gabe gathers the remaining pieces of his mug in his hands, and dumps them in the trash can as he turns away from the television.

"This place is *never* going to change. There's a hate that's deeply rooted here," he says.

"That's not true, babe. Theo and Travis and the Rev have been doing so much! Don't you think?" Chanel reaches for his arm, but he keeps walking into the bathroom to start his shower.

"So what's the topic for service this morning, anyway?"

Chanel walks away from the pastel yellow dress she's laid out on the bed and over to the dresser where her phone had been charging overnight.

"Let me see if they posted it on the church profile." She opens an app and begins to scroll a bit. "I know last week he said he was continuing his series on the Levels of Love. I really liked that one and I found some great resources we can use for our own follow-up session."

"I really can't believe I'm letting you turn me into a Bible study brat," Gabe complains as he steps out of the shower, dripping water onto the shaggy brown rug beneath him.

"Don't act like you weren't all into our session last week. Trying to tell me how Rev had his levels mixed up, and friendly love could never come after romantic love."

"It can't," he replies.

"You think he would be teaching these sermons if he didn't know what he was talking about?"

Gabe pokes his head out of the bathroom door, holding a toothbrush, mouth full of toothpaste, towel around his waist, and says, "Yes, I do, cause he doesn't know what he's talking about. How could I possibly have really and truly loved you romantically if I didn't love you first as a friend? That's called lust and is also the reason Reverend Brown is down on his wedding quota for the year."

She opens her mouth to protest but thinks about his statement.

"Don't trust everything these pastors say, babe," he adds with a smug grin, as he leans back into the bathroom. "God gave us brains to use too!"

"Whatever, Mr. Skeptic," she says, rolling her eyes. "Anyways, the sermon for today is… Oh! It's a celebration service for Theo," she says excitedly, happy to hear that their friend is being recognized. "They must be for all his work with the—" she stops.

"With the Peace Rally?" asks Gabe, stepping back into the bedroom as he's buttoning his crimson dress shirt.

"It says," she starts, choking with confusion, "it's 'A Celebration of Life service, honoring the life and legacy of Theophilus Monroe, who was—" Her eyes are locked on the phone in her hand, while she slowly raises her other hand to cover her mouth.

Gabe tilts his head to the left, examining her expression, "Babe, what is it?"

"Who was shot and killed in Central Park last night," she finishes as she plops onto the bed next to her dress. Gabe quickly moves to her side and wraps his arm around her.

"How could…? Who would…?" she attempts to ask trying to gather some semblance of reasoning. She pauses and cries to Gabe, "Just… Why Theo?"

Across town on the East side, Officer Bailey stands in the bedroom of a distraught Mayor Hilary Banks, who is sitting in an ornate chair, looking out at the New Locale from the window in her home asking the same question, as he briefs her on the situation.

"Why Theo?" She asks rubbing the temples of her forehead with her eyes closed. "Why, of all people him?"

"It was an accident, Mom," he answers bashfully.

Her eyes fling open. "Oh, I've heard that before," she snaps. "From you too many times, from your father, and it's *never* at the right time. This isn't going to help with the election! But I can't worry about that now. I'll reach out to the family to apologize and then I'll hold a press conference. You've really made a mess this time."

"I know. I'm sorry. When you do your address to the city I'll go apologize too, and—"

"Don't say a damn thing to anyone! Stay out of my way so I can deal with this properly. You've dishonored your badge with your behavior too many times. I'm suspending you indefinitely."

She gets up from her chair to head to the bathroom and get dressed.

Where Love Resides

"You can still make yourself useful and bring his friend Travis here. I'd like to talk to him about what he saw."

"But Mom," Bailey starts, "he's still on the West side. We don't have anyone who can cross over to get him."

"Oh, right. He does frequent that side of town, doesn't he," she states. "Well, you said something about a video, right? Has that gotten to the public?"

"No, we had the police tower scramble his cellular service to block anything going in or out."

"Okay, okay," she says, resting her hand over her heart. "So they don't know it's you yet. This curse has been a secret buried deep in New Locale's history. No one outside of here must know about what's going on. If anyone asks," she starts, "Just tell them it's another mistake by an officer, like all the rest in this country.

"You know, your father did what he had to do to fix his mistake, but I don't think you're capable of that. Don't leave this house." She mutters in a low voice, "This is exactly why I kept my maiden name."

She closes the door and as he watches her leave, he sees the picture of his mother and his son on the mantle. He remembers the shining eyes of the little boy, who would've

65

turned nine in a few months, pulls back his fist and lets it go flying into the wall beside the picture. He steps away from the hole he made, and stands by the window, looking out over the city with a piercing gaze filled with rage and pain.

IV

The ride to church is heavy and silent. Aside from the soft hum of the car engine and the steady sound of the tires against the pavement, neither Gabe nor Chanel make a sound as he drives. His eyes are locked on the street ahead of him, hands gripping the wheel at ten and two, focused, keeping his attention on anything but the thoughts of defeat, the thoughts of despair, or the thoughts of rage that are waiting to flood, like a dam cracked and ready to burst into his consciousness the second he acknowledges them. As long as he is distracted by the task of driving, he is cool. He turns on the radio, and the music stops as the DJ interrupts for a special message.

"Hey, Infinite family, I hate to cut the vibes," she says, "but I'm trying to keep y'all in the loop on what's going on out here. They *finally* confirmed that it was Theo who was killed, but we already knew that. They're still protecting police officer who shot him. Surprise, surprise, right? A few minutes ago, Mayor Banks took the steps of City Hall, the East side of the steps, to say this."

The mayor's voice comes over the radio. "It is with a heavy heart that I come before you all to send my apologies and condolences out to the community. I heard about the tragedy that's taken place and did not want to believe something like this could happen. I'm even more torn apart—" her voice cracks with emotion as she takes a pause. "—to learn that it was our beloved Theo who fell victim to this heinous crime. And at the hands of our own police department—the very ones we expect to keep us safe! This is wholly unacceptable!" she shouts in to the microphone. "We're still running an investigation to determine which officer is to be held responsible for this, but I want you all, residents of New Locale, to rest assured that justice will be served! 'Hashtag He Matters!' Thank you."

The DJ's voice returns. "That's right. Theo mattered. Don't let them forget! I'm playing this one, Aaliyah's 'We Need a Resolution' in honor of Theo. Rest in Power, young King."

Chanel gazes outside as she leans on the door beside her, resting her chin on her arm at the base of the window. Though her eyes remain fixed on the passing of the trees, the houses, and other sights along the road, she didn't see a thing.

She looks over at Gabe. "Babe," she starts, "All of these questions are just manifesting and repeating themselves in different ways in my head. Like, 'Why Theo? Why today? This isn't supposed to happen to someone like him. It doesn't make any sense. Why does this keep happening? 'Hashtag it doesn't matter'? I don't want Theo to be right about that, but—'"

The questions stop abruptly, as Gabe slams on the brakes and the car jerks them both out of their trances.

"Hey! What the hell is wrong with y'all?" he shouts at two small children, a Black boy and White boy, coming from the West side, who are standing frozen in the street. Their legs, coming out of loosely tied sneakers, are so close to the car that they must feel the heat radiating through the front grill of the engine.

"You need to watch where you're going!" Gabe yells.

Through the windshield, they see the White one mouth the word "Sorry," with big innocent brown eyes, as his friend picks up the posterboard they were carrying. He brushes it off, and after a brief inspection, they nod and run off in the direction of City Hall. Chanel catches a glimpse of the board. Clumsily painted in red, blue, and yellow are the words JUSTICE FOR THEO! #HEMATTERS. The midday sun is beginning to heat up the atmosphere of New Locale, and as the shock from the near accident mixes with the repressed frustrations of earlier, Gabe begins his verbal explosion.

"C'mon! They didn't even think about what they were doing. Who's letting them run out into the streets like this anyway? Someone needs to take blame! That weak-ass 'Sorry' won't cut it this time—"

"Babe!" Chanel interrupts. "Let it go. They're just kids!"

He looks at her and sighs, releasing the remaining anger for the moment. He gathers himself and recomposes as he lets his foot off the brake to keep driving.

After a few moments of silence, he says, "I wasn't really talking about the kids…"

When they arrive at the church, Gabe feels the hairs on Chanel's skin rise and goose bumps ripple down her arm. Before they can even walk up the steps they feel the emotion overflowing from the building. The moment Gabe grabs the handle of the heavy metal door, he knows he needs more than the usual strength to open not just the door, but also to prepare his mind and spirit for the tidal wave of Death's tsunami, raging with injustice, crashing against the metal as if pulsing through the handle and into the grip of his fist on it.

Once the door splits from its frame, the opening reveals every ounce of the flood waiting inside for them. Gabe grabs Chanel as she is almost knocked off her feet as the scene in the church comes into view. The first wave to hit them is heard, and it is carried in the voices of the hundred-something choir singers on stage. The sight of them alone, all dressed in white gowns, is overwhelming as the golden midday sunlight pours into the room through the twenty-foot windows that line the walls. Yet, it is the choir's collective voice that stops them in their tracks. Their song is an intense hymn of pain and passion that was so strong, so loud, the acoustics bounce off the church walls and straight into their eardrums. As the choir members wail into the air, with outstretched arms, fingers reaching for the heavens, and tears streaming down their sorrow-trodden faces, the vibrant organist beside them grimaces as he throws his head back and slams down on the keys. The lament vibrates through every inch of the building, shaking the floor and the feet that stand upon it, so that Gabe and Chanel feel their ribcages

71

rattle their hearts as they become part of the music. The choir's cry of emotion is so intense it feels as though their voices are hands grabbing at their audience's throats and pulling at the vocal cords of everyone in the congregation, who gasp, scream, cry, and exhale their own unsung cries of pain. This song is a collective expression of grief.

The choir song turns into a heavy hum as they take their seats, and the rest of the church does the same. An usher directs Gabe and Chanel to one of the pews. On any other day they would sit closer to the front of the church, but so many people have come to the service today that they have to find seats in one of the last rows. When they finally sit down, Gabe surveys the room. The organ is still playing along with the hum of the choir, and the congregation continues their weeping as well.

One woman in the third row has remained standing, violently swings her head from side to side as she cries out to the ceiling. Her swinging comes to a stop as she begins to make several slow, steady, strong jumps in place, her fists balled up at her side, her body rippling with pain each time. After the last jump she raises a hand into the air and shouts unintelligibly in tongues that no one recognizes, but are understood by all, as someone else echoes her cries asking "Why, Lord? Why, Lord? Oh why?"

Where Love Resides

In several places around the church, groups of five or six people are gathered in circles around one person who is on their knees or lying outstretched on the floor crying. The others lay hands on them or fan them with paper programs that bear Theo's face, as they send words of prayer asking, "God, bring this person all the peace and serenity they may need in this time! Let them know Your Will is present at *all* times, and they *will* make it through the days, minutes, hours, years, and lifetimes that should follow this great tragedy, Lord!"

Gabe looks down at Chanel resting her head on his shoulder, hoping to find a better view, only to catch a glimpse of an older woman far off in the corner of the room. She is dressed in black from head to toe, with a wide-brimmed black hat that covers her face from the nose up. But the hat is sitting at an angle that reveals just enough of her face for Gabe to see the single teardrop roll down her cheek and fall into her firmly pressed lips. She sways a cardstock fan before her that is all white, except for a large black '#' sign on it.

Trying to take in everything that is going on, Gabe closes his eyes and rubs his forehead.

This is too much, he thinks.

Ashley A.T.

With his eyes still closed, flashbacks of his father's funeral service, which took place in the very same church, arise in his mind. He sees that younger version of himself, sitting on the side of the stage with Marcus and their mother, wide-eyed and afraid of knowing a new world without his father, as the casket lay in front of them. He opens his eyes, coming back to the present and fighting away the past, before the tears can well up inside. When he does, his sight follows his memories to the side of the stage, where he now sees Theo's face sitting in a beautiful ornate from next to his family, along with Travis, who has the same "This is too much" expression on his face, his eyes swollen and as red as his hair. Gabe shakes his head with his eyes narrowed and brows furrowed.

*What's he doing up there, with the **family**,* he thinks. *And for all that posing and talking he does online any other day, he sure as hell been quiet for a **manager**!*

Chanel, as if she can hear his thoughts, places her hand on his leg and firmly taps it to draw his attention away from the anger inside. It does, and he wraps his arm around her so he can hold her close. But the moment of peace she gave him is quickly interrupted as everyone stands to see Reverend Brown at the door to the side of the altar. His face is empty of bright, inviting smile that he usually bears.

Where Love Resides

Today his mouth is turned down in a frown that falls with the wrinkles of his skin, and his eyes are cold, robbed of their energetic glow of life, darkened under his low eyebrows. Draped in a royal purple and gold robe made of a thick, luscious velvet that cascades onto the floor around his feet, he pauses at the doorway before he begins to walk. The ends of the robe drag behind him as he moves across the stage at a crawling pace. His long, slow steps appear drawn out not for dramatic effect or due to the heaviness of his robe, but because he is weighed down with the feat of preparing to deliver a sermon that he isn't sure he is emotionally or spiritually equipped to deliver. About halfway to the podium, he stops in his tracks when he catches sight of Travis, whose his red eyes meet his own, silently asking the reverend "Why?" The preacher shakes his head and exhales a breath that silently replies "Son, I can't begin to tell you." He clutches the gold-encased bible he carries to his chest, takes a deep breath and makes his final steps to begin to speak.

"Please," he starts, "be seated if you can. Brothers and Sisters, there's no need for me to introduce the subject I'm forced to speak on today, for I know we all can feel the great loss that's taken place and affected our community in the hours that have passed since last night. I know I feel it…"

"We feel it, Reverend!" someone calls out.

"Yes, I feel it when I look out into this congregation before me, and I don't see the smiling face, with his bright, innocent eyes, who for the last twenty-two years sat faithfully in the third row of this middle aisle in front of me—" He holds his hand out to the empty seat. "—where he, like a sponge, took in the good Lord's word with more eagerness and dedication than folks two and three times his age since the time he was small enough to run around the church grounds. And even then, he lived the message in every step he made."

He pauses as his mind seems to follow the memory.

"I feel it when I look beside me, and I see his face immortalized in this beautiful frame, far, far too soon for it to feel right, instead of sitting next to his brother in the Spirit. The sight of him without Travis, or Travis without him—" He looks at Travis for a moment, then quickly looks away and continues in a strained voice. "It's unsettling."

The church is quiet.

"To know that New Locale will never again see these two young men united in their fight for the good is something that my mind can't even comprehend right now, and frankly, I'm not sure it ever will."

Chanel presses her hand over her heart as the tears roll down her face, and Gabe pulls her closer to him.

"I feel it," the reverend goes on, "when I think about yesterday, and how Theo proclaimed himself as 'Hashtag It Doesn't Matter'. Huh." He laughs as he looks down shaking his head. "It doesn't matter…?" He raises his head and gazes out into the church. "I look at all of these saddened faces of all ages and races that have come to pay respects to this young man and I think… 'It doesn't matter'?" He steps beside the podium. "I just came from the storage room downstairs, where we brought the piles and piles of donations that were referred to as '*trash*'," he says with disgust, "that we know are a symbol of *love* that Theo asked us to show, and I think… 'It doesn't matter'?"

"Preach, pastor!" someone shouts.

"Look at all the good he's done for this community!" Reverend Brown roars into the microphone, eyes bulging with rage as sweat glistens from his face. "What a shame! A shame that young Theo thought that his name did not matter. But," he holds the microphone close to his face and points toward the window, "I want you all to take a minute to look

77

outside. Do you see what's out there? That ethereal wave of light, the Curse of the Red Sea, is God's way of letting us know that Theophilus Monroe the Third, mattered and matters still!"

"Amen!" numerous people call out, as the congregation begins to stand and clap.

Reverend Brown is standing at the edge of the altar, leaning over so far it's a miracle itself that he did not fall off as he speaks.

"Now, I was just a young boy when the curse fell upon us last time, but let me tell you what I learned about it!"

"Tell it, Reverend!"

"You see, if you're familiar with the story of Moses, you'll recall how, when he was doing the good Lord's work—" He heaves a deep breath while wiping the sweat from his head. "—he led His people to the Red Sea as they were being persecuted!"

"Yes, he did!"

"And now you'll remember," he gasps again, "that when they had nowhere to turn Moses stuck his staff into the water and the mighty Lord split that ocean into two! And if I do recall correctly, I seem to remember that as Moses helped his followers cross that ocean floor, when the villainous

Pharaoh Ramses had his army follow them, his soldiers were washed away and drowned in the raging waters on that day!"

"They surely were!"

"C'mon, now!"

The reverend strides to the other side of the stage and wipes his sweat again as he says, "So now it would seem that this curse has returned to tell us something."

"What's it here for?"

"Let us know!"

"If you *believe*" he drags out his last word and points out into the congregation, "that Theo was doing what's righteous here among us, then I think you will agree that he was the Moses of New Locale. And just as I'm standing here, it would seem that this city has been split in two, has it not?"

"Yes, it has, Pastor!"

"Now the Red Sea represents the precious blood of our savior Jesus Christ, in which through the baptism our sins are drowned, just as Moses' enemies were brought to death by water for refusing to accept the Lord's Word into their heart." He moves back to the podium. "But for those who have surrendered—" He inhales noisily. "Even if you sit here and don't practice this religion, those who are

79

conscious in their mind and spirit of the nature and destiny of man in the universe—" He gasps again. "By simply doing what's right, you shall know, from now until the end of time, *peace*! You shall know *love* in all of their days!" he shouts. "And when the time should come that our bodies can no longer dwell here on Earth, we shall not have to ask where we will spend eternity, for our souls will rise up, high above the clouds, and be drawn into the *light*!" he bellows, throwing head back and tossing his hands into the air.

"*Hallelujah*!" the people shout.

"Glory to God!" someone cries out.

As everyone sends wails of praise and rejoicing, as the choir chimes in with an angelic "*Ahhhhhh-mennnnn*!" and the organist strikes the chords to match. After a few moments, everyone is quiet. Reverend Brown, having had enough time to catch his breath and resume his composed position at the podium, begins his closing remarks.

"Now I want to invite anyone here who feels compelled to dedicate themselves to the Lord to come forth at the end of service and become a sustaining member of the New Bethel Baptist Church today. Here we learn to come together under one roof, to take fellowship with one another, so that we may do so every day in our city as well. I say this because coming together is the only way for us to heal, to break the curse that has plagued our community for too long. At this time I would like to bring up a young man who I think exemplifies this sense of unity. Travis—" He turns to face him. "Would you come say a few words?"

Everyone cheers and applauds, eager for the enthusiastic vigor they've come to expect from Travis's speeches.

But the freckled young man looks up at the reverend from his seat with tired eyes and says, "Not today, Rev."

Reverend Brown's face falls, and a cloud of disappointed sighs fill the air, weighing down the room.

"Poor Travis," Chanel says.

Gabe glances at her, annoyed with disbelief, and kisses his teeth at her remark. "I'm not buying it," he says.

She pulls away from his arm, "So, you don't think he might be a little too upset to talk after he just lost his best friend?"

He's on his feet before she finishes her question and shouts, "Oh, so now the 'loud-mouth White boy' who thinks it's his job to speak for the West side has nothing to say?"

Chanel turns, hiding her face with embarrassment, as low murmurs escape the mouths of the congregation, seeds of suspicion and question aimed towards the front of the church. Travis remains still in his seat, aside from the red fist he clenches tightly.

"Yeah, that's what I thought," Gabe calls out. "Theo's *manager* was only riding for the West side when he could get something out of it! What we got to offer you now that you can't have your client usher you into our neighborhood?"

Travis's eyes spring open wide, ready to dispute the accusations. He pushes himself out of his seat, but takes his time walking to the podium.

When he reaches it, he leans into the microphone and simply says, "Don't let them trick you into dividing us even further, that's exactly what they want." He closes his eyes as if collecting himself.

"Reverend Brown is right, we *all* have to come together, and right now. Seeing all of you here today tells me that you understand what Theo was trying to do. I just can't get past the conversation I had with him before—" He chokes back a sob.

"He was telling me how he didn't think he mattered, and I tried to argue with him, but this tragedy happened and… It's devastating to know that he's gone, but the real tragedy is that he was right. He doesn't matter."

There's a gasp as the voices of the congregation rise with hurt and shock at his words.

"I know, I know how it sounds, but think about it. Last night I looked up all of the names of the men, the women, and the children, unjustly killed by police in cities across America, and I was *disgusted*!" His voice rises now. "I read the news articles about them. I looked at the comments of support from friends and family, who seemed hurt, but not surprised. I read the insidious mocking and condemnation from wicked people who saw nothing wrong with what they were witnessing, and that's when I realized that Theo was right. It doesn't matter how many peace rallies he held. It doesn't matter that he was educated and trying to get his master's in civil engagement from the university. It doesn't matter what he did for us, because there's nothing he could have done that would have changed the color of his skin or the fact that he was an expendable pawn, another victim, in the system of racism and oppression that they enforce in our communities!

"I heard what they've been saying on the news about me being Theo's manager, and I find it oddly coincidental that I can't get a signal on my phone to publicly refute any of their statements. I don't know what they're trying to get you to believe, but I can only hope that you know the true nature of our friendship. Since I can't share this, I'd like to ask you all to please take out your phones and record this, because..." He pauses. "Because although it's clear that Theo did not matter to Officer Brandon Bailey of the New Locale Police Department, or to the mayor, who is aware and covering for her son, Theo mattered to me and I'll be damned if he dies with this truth hidden away!"

The blinds over the large windows fall and the room darkens as he points to the projector screen behind him. Then, the video he recorded begins to play for everyone to see. The screen shows Theo's bleeding body rising between the columns of light. The congregation gasps as they watch, many of them seeing the curse's wrath play out for the first time with their own eyes. The video quickly shifts from the image of Theo to Officer Bailey, standing behind the barrier across from where Travis records.

"Come closer!" Travis calls. "Here you all have seen the truth! Do with this information as you must. Do whatever you have to do to share this with the world and let them know! 'Hashtag He Matters!'" he shouts, throwing his fist into the air.

The people rush from their seats to capture the moment on their phones and join in the chanting.

Where Love Resides

Chanel is just getting her phone out of her purse when Gabe pulls her arm, dragging her into the aisle, and out the doors of the church. "We're not sticking around to watch this," he tells her, quickly brushing his other hand across his face to wipe the tear that falls from his eye.

She follows behind him, silently, yet as the noon sun catches their eyes while they walk to the car, it sparks a flame that will begin to boil a rage in everyone who stands in its light.

V

Gabe drives along the familiar streets again, but the car ride back from church is nothing like their ride there. The melancholy silence has been replaced by a passionately furious discussion.

"What do you mean, 'There's absolutely nothing we can do,' Gabe? How could you even dare to say something like that after Rev—"

"He's bullshitting y'all and he knows it! It's his job to give people that sense of false hope to 'go on another day' and 'make a change'. He's getting paid off that hope! He's seen New Locale suffer with this curse before, and you best believe he'll collect as many new member fees at the church as he can. As a matter of fact, he sports one of those new robes every time this happens. Plus he's got Travis up there trying to recruit from the East side now too."

"Travis isn't on the East side right now! He's here trying to do something right. I don't know if I can say the same for you."

"Oh, I'll tell you what he's right about. He sees that Theo's life didn't matter, so now he's going to run up under Rev to have his voice heard. He's thinking about himself, like the rest of us need to. If everything Theo did for everyone else couldn't help him and hasn't changed a thing here, there's not a thing you and I can do except make sure we good. And we need to find something else to do with that degree of yours, cause it damn sure ain't going to help us get out of here."

"Stop the car!" Chanel demands, pulling on the door handle.

Gabe brings the car to a halt and watches her rage, so frustrated she can't focus enough to actually pull up the door lock the first few times she grabs it to get the door open.

"I don't need to be around your negativity! That's that stuck-on-the-past mindset that's going to keep you from being part of the change the rest of us are creating. Just because the past hurt you doesn't mean I'm going to let it slow me down!"

"So you think you can walk home faster than I can drive?" Gabe forces his voice to stay calm an even, partly because he knows it infuriates her.

"I'll have a *better* walk alone, on the path to peace, than letting you crush my spirit the way you've let the world crush yours!"

"Yeah, well maybe you'll find a reality check on your *long* three-block journey home. I'll be waiting there to hear the tale!" He throws his head back to laugh.

"How you getting in, Gabe?" she asks, pulling two silver keys from her purse.

He looks at the lonely car key sitting in the ignition and remembers that he gave her the key to go back upstairs as they were leaving when he forgot his wallet.

"Yeah, I thought so!" She taunts. "I don't care where you go, but don't come back around me with those bad vibes. How's that for a reality check?"

All he can do is stare, bitterly, as she walks off, giving the keys a mocking jingle before tossing them in her purse. She makes a little skip in her step to show she is remaining upbeat and positive, but Gabe can see the tears welling up in her eyes. She reaches to wipe her cheek just as Gabe pulls past her. He turns left as she turns right, hoping that by going in the opposite direction she won't think he is hurt by her words. He clicks on the radio just as another update from DJ MMS is on.

"So if you haven't been online, the video from Travis Phillips's phone is now being shared around the city. We just heard that a riot was ready to break out on the steps of City Hall between residents on the East and West sides, but no one could get through the Curse's wave. Mayor Banks hasn't come forth since this morning, but people are lining up on both sides of City Hall, demanding answers. That barrier won't be there all day now, y'all. If it follows suit from last time, back in the sixties, it's only a matter of time before it's gone, and we *have* to come together. I'll keep y'all in the know on what's going on, and," she snapped her fingers, "as a matter of fact, I'm about to spin this Marvin Gaye 'What's Going On'! I know we might be angry and confused, but remember '*War is not the answer, for only Love can conquer hate.*' Keep the peace, y'all."

The horns blow as the song begins, and Gabe turns the volume up a bit. It was one of his father's favorite songs. His mind drifts to the past as he cruises down the street. He sees his younger self, Marcus, and his father, Moses, riding in that very same car the day they bought it, brand new off of the lot. As Gabe sat in the passenger seat, he was about to pop a disk in the CD player, when his father quickly held out his hand to stop him.

"What you doing with that? We have the radio, son!"

"The radio? Dad, that's old school. You never know what they're going to play, and I don't like my music being interrupted by commercials."

"That's the beauty of it though! We're in this car now because of the sale I heard about on the radio. You get to be surprised by whatever you hear. Plus, these New Locale radio waves carry the truth. They know exactly what you need to hear, when you need to hear it, and you might be blocking your blessing by being stuck in your ways. Watch this. Hey Marcus, I'll give you five dollars if you can tell me what you're listening to!"

A young Marcus, sitting in the backseat, didn't respond. He was bobbing his head with his eyes closed and ears covered, blasting music through the headphones he was wearing.

"See, now that boy just missed his blessing!"

"Yeah, whatever, Dad. I bet whatever comes on this radio ain't half as good as this new Nelly album that dropped. That 'Hot in Herre' is hot for real!"

"All right, that's a bet."

He clicks the radio on and "What's Going On" is playing.

"Now that's what I'm talking about!" Moses yelps.

"Nah, Dad. You lost this one. This 'cry me a river' song ain't going to get no party started."

"You're absolutely right. You need to listen deeper, son. I was just a boy, half your age, when Marvin Gaye wrote this, but anyone could see that he was trying to get us to take a stand against the hate and racial tension sweeping the nation back then."

"Well, he didn't do a good job. We still get profiled and discriminated against every day."

"We had a classmate get lynched in Central Park '71, son. It literally split the city in two. I know New Locale is behind in a lot of ways, but don't think that things can't get better. Just look around, really look and pay attention to what's going on around you, and like the song says, '*Find a way to bring some lovin here today!*' You hear me, son?"

He heard him. He heard him then, and the words still ring true as he comes out of his daydream just in time to brake hard before he hits the kid crossing the street in front of him. It's one of the boys from earlier that ran in front of them on their way to church, the White kid. He is alone as he walks, robbed of his vigor and eager sprint from before, dragging his feet in shoes with untied laces sprawled on the street, hanging his head down as his loose brown curls fall over his face. He barely acknowledges Gabe's car, just a few inches away from his small body. He just peers over from the corner of his eye and continues his persistently slow, sad march across the street.

Gabe puts his car in park and is ready to jump out to deliver a heavy-handed lecture to the child, but he hears the song still playing as Marvin sings, *"Don't punish me with brutality. Talk to me, so you can see..."* He pauses as he lets the message settle. He closes his eyes and takes a deep breath, before he grabs the door handle and steps outside.

"Hey, kid," he calls out in a cool, gentle voice, as he walks to the front of the car to lean against the hood.

Startled, the boy looks up a Gabe with a curious, but cautious expression.

"What's going on? You lose your favorite teddy bear at the playground today or something?" Gabe asks, with a serious look of concern before his friendly smile and charm make their appearance.

The boy, now distracted from his worries, smiles a half-amused smile, and answers. "Sir, I'm eight-and-three-quarters years old. See?" He displays eight of his fingers and then pulls three quarters out of his pocket. "I'm too old for teddy bears," he announces proudly, showing his snaggle-toothed grin.

"Oh, my bad, boss," Gabe replies, holding up his hands. "So what's bothering you, then? 'Cause this is the *second* time you've stepped in front of my car today. I would hate to have interrupted any of your important eight-and-three-quarters-years-old activities with a trip to the hospital."

"*Oh!* I'm sorry, mister," says the boy, looking apologetic with big, shining green eyes. "Me and my best friend, Donny Carmichael, who's only eight-and-a-half—" He holds up his fingers and uses two quarters this time. "— were trying to hurry to get to the justice march for Mr. Theo. He used to donate toys to our school and come read to us, so me and Donny ran to City Hall so we could get the posters we made for him on TV, and we did! He was watching on the TVs in heaven."

"So," Gabe says impatiently, "what's wrong then?"

"Well, my dad was watching from my grandma's house, and when he saw me on TV he ran out so fast! He was yelling, 'Austin! Austin, get over here!', but he couldn't get to me because he was on the East side and I was on the

Ashley A.T.

West, and then everyone started screaming and yelling and pushing each other, so I couldn't get to him either. He looked mad, probably because I was with Donny and he doesn't have any Black friends and talks bad, saying mean things about anyone Black and—"

"*Whoa, whoa*," Gabe interrupts, standing up from the car. "Timeout, lil man. Austin, you said?"

"Yeah, but my friends call me AB. And since I'm going to be turning nine in a quarter of months, I'm thinking about changing it to something cool like 'AB-3000' or—"

"All right, AB. First of all, slow down. Second, what is a little Eastside kid with a dad that doesn't like us doing over here? How'd you cross over here anyways?"

"Oh, me and Donny play on both sides of New Locale all the time! Usually no one can see us though. He didn't have any friends to play with before we met, so we're always together and looking out for each other. I was sad because we got separated when everyone was pushing at the march. I heard my grandma say that my dad used to have a friend who looked like Donny when he was my age, but he got hurt and my granddad that I never met had to take him away and they never came back. My dad was so mad that he got upset at anyone who looked like his friend, and that's why he's still so mean now. I hope I don't grow up angry

94

like my dad. I should go to my grandma's house to talk to him. She lives at 1810 East Main Street. It's the big blue house past Central Park, with the swing on the corner. I like to play and run around in the yard and it's great, cause—"

"Hey, Austin," Gabe interjects. "You want a ride? I can't go to the East side, but I can get you close so you're not running in the streets. You can tell me about all your fun on the way there."

"I'm not supposed to get in cars with strangers."

"Well, you've basically given me your whole family history and address. I'll tell you my story on the way there. I'm Gabe, by the way."

"Can you tell me why you were fighting with your girlfriend, Mr. Gabe?"

"Wife!" Gabe quickly corrects him. "And no. That's grown folks business, and none of your business even if you were grown."

"Actually the emotions that are present in everyone's homes affect the community," Austin recites, "because they can build up little by little and then manifest on a larger scale. That's what Mr. Theo taught us. I hope that you're not very angry at your wife. But that's probably why you can't cross to the East, because your heart isn't right!"

Gabe blinks and stares at Austin, taken aback by the truth and seriousness of his statement. He thinks about it for a moment. He sees Chanel's face in his mind and he smiles.

"Naw, I'm not that angry with her. I could never be. She lit a fire in my heart that melted away all my cold nights and her face brightens up even my darkest days. I love her too much to be mad."

"Well then, Mr. Gabe," Austin starts, glowing in admiration of his declaration of affection, "I think you should go tell her that you love her. Mr. Theo said that the little good feelings we have can lead to bigger ones, and fix the bad if we use them. So you better do something real nice for your wife to fix your fight with her."

"How do you know so much about love, lil man?"

"I told you, I'm eight-and-three-quarters years old. I've seen a lot of things!"

"Yeah, well your wisdom earned you another quarter. Happy Birthday," Gabe says as he pulls a quarter out of his pocket, and flips it to Austin.

"Wow, thanks, Mr. Gabe! I gotta tell my dad he owes me a birthday cake!"

"Let me grab my cellphone so you can give him a call," he says.

As he turns around to walk to the car door, he hears little *clink, clink, clink, clink!* sounds.

"Austin?"

He looks around but doesn't see the child anywhere. He walks around the car, then turns in a circle to scan the area around him, but he's nowhere in sight. He returns to the front of the car, where a glimmer of light catches his eye. He looks down to see a broken shoelace and four quarters on the ground where they were standing, with two quarters on the left of the shoelace and the other two on the right. He picks up the shoelace and tosses it away, and suddenly the four quarters turn a fiery red color. He stomps on them with his shoe, then blows on them and watches as the red turns to a cool blue, and the quarters begin to melt together as one coin. He waits in astonishment, then picks up the coin after it hasn't changed for a while, flipping it over in his hand he reads each side.

"It. Matters." the coin reads. The reverse side says, "We. Matter."

"What the hell is going on today?" Gabe shakes his head, trying to clear away the confusion of the moment.

Slipping the coin in his pocket, he suddenly feels a longing for his wife, his sense of peace in moments like this.

Thinking about Austin's words again, he gets in the car and turns down West Main Street, deciding to make one more stop before he heads home.

VI

Chanel's been back at the apartment for some time now, still very upset by the fight. On any other Sunday, she would come home from church and head straight to the kitchen to start their Sunday dinner, while Gabe would fold the laundry they let wash before they left, after he'd step out on their balcony for a smoke. They see their marriage as a partnership. Both of them glad to do all they can to keep each other happy. But right now, she doesn't care about any of that. She is mad. Out of habit, she has gone straight to the kitchen like she did normally, but instead of floating around, daintily placing pots and pans and delicately dicing and assembling the ingredients of their meal, she furiously slams her cookware onto the stove and carelessly throws the food into the oven, swearing and cursing her husband's name as she prepares dinner.

Ashley A.T.

"I can't believe I have to walk around with this dumbass man's last name for the rest of my life!" she exclaims out loud while fervently chopping onions on the cutting board. "What was I thinking, letting him sweep me off my naive little feet? Wait, wait, no. What was *he* thinking saying that bullshit to me in the car? That son of a—oh, he's lucky his mother is such a sweet lady and I don't want to curse her name, but *he* can go to h-e-l-l for all I care right now!"

Her eyes begin to burn and tear up as her vision becomes blurry, but she keeps chopping.

"Stupid onions," she says in a shaky voice as she wipes her eyes, chopping the them harder. "Stupid Gabe starting that stupid fight. Stupid police doing the opposite of their job. Stupid world with all this hate tearing us apart little by little every day. Stupid, stupid, stupid. This is all so stupid. *Ow!*"

She screams as the knife cuts into her finger. She drops it and gives into her emotions, letting go and plopping on the ground as she sobs. Her phone rings. She takes a deep breath and a moment to gather herself before she answers.

"Hey, Angela," she says in a quiet voice.

"Sis! Are you okay? Your city is all on the news! The park, the march turned brawl at City Hall, and now they're talking about a riot planned for tonight? What's going on?"

"Riot? I'm fi-fine." Her voice cracks, revealing her distressed disposition.

"Oh, Cha…" her sister replies. "You don't sound fine. I know you and Gabe were close with Theo. Is Gabe working today? Is he there with you?"

"I don't know where he is. We, uh—" She hesitates. "We had a fight on the way home from church and I walked home."

"Gabe let you *walk home*? Do I need to come drive out there and check him for you? I know you're probably in there sitting on the floor crying your eyes out."

Chanel pushes herself up off the ground before she speaks. "No, I'm not! I've learned better than to let his pessimism get to me by now."

"Yeah, and I bet the fight started over what y'all can do, if anything, to heal from this?"

"How'd you know?"

"Girl, I know how these things work. Times like this always bring out the worst in even the best of us. The same thing happened with me and John when they arrested that

101

college student because she was 'reading for free' in a coffee shop." Chanel could practically hear her sister rolling her eyes on the other end. "John was talking about, 'If they're offering *free* WiFi, then she shouldn't have to pay to use it and has every right to be there!' Hmm, let a trick roll up in my house for some 'free' air conditioning without putting in for this very un-free electric bill and see if we don't have a problem! Okay?" she concluded with a snap of her fingers.

"You sound just as selfish and self-centered as Gabe. I'm ashamed to call you my sis."

"Oh, shut up! You know you love me, and Gabe is still the man you fell in love with. Watch, he's probably on his way back with something for you so y'all can hug, kiss, and have some bomb-ass make-up sex, *haha*!"

"Really, Ange?"

"Hell yeah! Don't act like I'm not right. That's how me and John got these twins over here now. I used to pick fights just to make up later. Now, we barely have time to throw a shady remark at each other before one of the boys starts crying." She lets out a sigh. "Enjoy your honeymoon phase while you can, girl."

"We'll see if you're right. I don't even want him to look at me right now! How are the twins, by the way? Send me some pics when you get a chance."

Where Love Resides

"Let me do that *right* now while they're sleeping so peacefully in one place finally. Mom was just asking me for some before she saw the news and told me to make sure you're not planning to join that riot later. But you'll probably be deep in love-after-war mode by then, if you know what I mean."

"Wait, what riot are you talking about? For Theo?"

Chanel hears the babies start to cry on the other line. "*Ugh!*" Angela shouts. "There goes the rest of my Sunday chill. Yeah, stop crying and turn on the news. Be safe, and tell Gabe I said the twins need a cousin! I gotta go."

"But wait—"

The phone clicks off. Chanel presses the remote to turn on the TV and leans on the counter. The anchorwoman giving a recap of the City Hall incident.

"Robin Reed here, reporting live for New Locale News at 5:32 PM. Just a little while ago we saw a peaceful protest almost turn into a violent disaster. We've since had a chance to interview some of the residents who were there. Here with me right now is Marcus Mathis, from West New Locale, who was front and center when it all went down. Marcus, can you tell us what happened here?"

103

Ashley A.T.

Marcus snatches the mic away from the newscaster.
"Yeah, let me tell you what's going on. Them hating-ass
Eastsiders tried to shut us down! They're protecting that
bully Bailey." He stops his story to spit on the ground. "But
y'all can't keep him away forever. We know *exactly* who
thought Theo didn't matter, but we gon' show y'all just how
much he mattered to the rest of us. We're matching that
energy as soon as that Red Sea wave is gone, and that's all I
gotta say about that."

He drops the microphone on the ground and raises his
fist in the air as he struts off until he's out of the camera's
sight. The anchorwoman bends down to pick it up, but a
hand appears and reaches it before she does. Marcus steps
back into the frame and brushes it off as he hands the
microphone back to her and mouths "Call me" with a smile
before he continues his march into the background of the
park.

With an annoyed look on her face she starts, "Um,
thank you, Marcus. Yes, that was about the scene from the
West side of City Hall. We haven't been able to get anyone
else to the East side to get a report from our other residents
since this morning, but like Marcus said, the Curse of the
Red Sea will not keep us apart forever. In fact, according to
our investigation, we can see that the barrier is slowly

dissolving as the distance between the two sides has already decreased from six feet apart to only three. Reports and documentation from the past lead us to believe that it will be gone by just about sundown. We're hoping that will bring some closure to this tragically eventful day here in New Locale, but it appears that many residents are lining up and preparing for some sort of a battle as soon as they can get to the other side of town.

"People, we are asking you to please get home and stay home this evening. Mayor Banks is asking you all to find it in your hearts to forgive the police department for their past mistakes and allow *them* to deal with any action taking place this evening. From the steps of City Hall, this is Robin Reed signing off."

As soon as the report ends, Chanel thinks of Gabe. "*God, please bring him home,*" she prays. "*I hope he gets back before the sun goes down. I can be mad at him after I know he's safe.*" She gasps at another thought. "*What if he goes out there alone? I don't want him fighting the world, but I damn sure don't want him fighting by himself either.*"

She walks to the balcony and steps outside. As she watches the sun begin its descent in the orange sky, she says, "I need to be with him."

"I need to get back to her," Gabe says.

Standing in the candy aisle of Seven Corners Convenience store, where the news report is just ending on the TV above him, he holds two packs of bright colored candies in his hands.

Two packs of these should get me back in her good graces, he thinks. *It's not like I was wrong, anyway. We just see things differently. But this is her favorite candy. It'll put that smile on her face that I fall in love with and everything will be right again. She's gotta know I'm always thinking about her.*

He surveys the aisle, weighing all of his candy-apology options, and as he turns his head to the right, he sees Mrs. Yamassee as she climbs up a stepping-stool to hang a poster at the store entrance. She reaches up to tie the top end, but her foot misses a step, and Gabe drops the candy and is at her side in an instant before she falls to the ground.

"I got you, Mrs. Y! Here, let me put this up for you."

"Oh, thank you my Gabe! I had no business trying to get up there with these old frail bones."

He hangs the poster, then steps down to look at it. The poster reads in a big, blue bold font, "Announcing the Seven

Corners #HeMatters Scholarship Fund," with a picture of a smiling Theo posed in the middle of all seven of the store clerks.

"Only Theo could get all y'all together at once," says Gabe. "Was this something you guys had planned before…"

"Yes!" She beams. "He was like a grandson to us here. He even took it up to learn how to say Grandma and Elder in each of our native tongues. He was always here buying snacks and supplies for his events. We were going to wait to announce the project, but we thought this would be a good way to do our part in keeping him alive."

"You mean like, to keep his legacy alive?"

"No! I mean keep him alive!" She snaps. "Death doesn't end a life if we don't let it. A man only dies when the living forget his legacy. And much he's left of a legacy and the things he did! But this," she says looking at his face on the banner, "this is what he *is* doing through us still. He's still with us."

Gabe studies the picture too. Theo's smile is so vibrant it looks as if he might start laughing, as if he is right there in the flesh. And as he stares, for just a moment the picture comes to life and Theo does laugh one of his cheerful laughs. Gabe jumps, startled, and turns to Mrs. Yamassee to see if she heard it, but she is facing the other direction, bearing a mischievous smile on her face.

"So, young Gabe, speaking of doing, what are you doing here, and most importantly, what are you doing here without Ms. Chanel for your usual post-Sunday service stop?"

Gabe is silent, embarrassed at being caught by her keen sense for things out of place.

"Oh, we just had a little fight," he replies. "Nothing serious, but she was pretty upset and walked home. I thought I'd get her some candy to make things right."

"Ah, I knew it! That candy aisle has seen many men ponder its shelves for a solution to their marital problems."

"Which one will get the job done?"

"None of them!" she cackles in a piercing laugh. "You aim to sugarcoat a bigger problem, my friend. And when you do that, you let the sugar invite insects into your house, and it's hard to get those bugs out once they've infested your home."

Gabe shrugs. "I see things my way, and she sees them in her own. She might be right about whatever she's seeing, but I'm not wrong either. I don't know what she wants."

The old woman takes a magazine off the rack next to her and gives his head a good smack. He ducks. "Hey!"

Where Love Resides

When he lifts his head, Mrs. Yamassee is gone, but in her place is Ms. Bajamo. With her head intricately wrapped in a colorful scarf, she gazes at him with a look as fierce as her accent is thick, yet her words are very clear.

"You know exactly what she wants! You just are not willing to give it to her. Black man, you must be willing to find compromise in your home, or you will find trouble about you in all of your days."

"I'm not giving up my reasonable understanding that's grounded in the truth, to placate her idealistic fantasies."

He feels a smack across his head again, and Mrs. Xiao is standing before him.

"*Ah!* You're not so bright as you think you are, Mr. Gabe. Show me your fist" she says quickly. He holds out his hand with his fingers balled up. "These are your beliefs, your experiences and understandings. Now catch!" She tosses him a candy bar, and he opens his hand to catch it.

"Now look at your hand. You opened your closed fist, your closed mind, to receive something new, something you couldn't have caught holding onto your own opinions."

"Okay, you might have given me something new, but I needed those *facts* and real life experiences, not opinions and metaphoric candy, to know how to catch."

"Put your right hand behind your back and catch again!"

She grabs a glass snowglobe from the counter this time and tosses them at Gabe then quickly throws another one behind it. He catches the first one, but the second one falls to the ground and shatters at his feet.

"Too bad you didn't have a second hand. A pretty hand, attached to your pretty wife perhaps, who could help you catch more than what you can alone. And now you have to buy a broken snowglobe. *Ha!*" She cackles into the air. "Let me go find a broom to sweep this up."

Gabe stands there bemused, reflecting on the words of the wise old women, when he hears the sound of a fist tearing through paper. He spins around to see two university students walking out of the store laughing, and a hole in the banner where Theo's face was. He is about to charge after them when he hears a familiar voice call his name.

"Gabe!" Marcus walks out of one of the aisles in the store. "You in here getting ready for battle too?" He's coming from the aisle with the grilling supplies, carrying a pack of matches and a bottle of lighter fluid.

"What? No, I gotta get home to Cha," Gabe says. "Man, what are you doing with this?"

"I'm waiting for that Red Curse to clear up, and then I'm heading to the East side to do a little clearing up of my own. C'mon, grab some gear and meet me in the park."

"Marcus, what are you talking about? You can't go burning down the city. That's not going to do anything but get you locked up, or worse."

"Man, we supposed to be New Locale soldiers. I'm willing to do what it takes to show them that all this they got going on, the deception and corruption, the racism, gotta come to an end. We were kids when they took Dad out and told us we couldn't—"

"Hey, man, we still can't talk about that."

"I don't care about that! Us keeping quiet about their dirt all these years is what keeps shit like this going on! We got an army ready to fight this time, and I hope you're part of it, cause you starting to sound like a punk, bro." He turns to leave. On his way out, he sees the poster with Theo's face punched in.

"See, we even got ones on this side disrespecting us! But all that is coming to an end." He walks out of the store.

111

Mrs. Yamassee finishes sweeping up the last of the glass on the floor and meets Gabe at the counter.

"I'll ring you up for the snowglobe, *and* the items that your brother just walked out with."

He pulls the wallet out of his pocket and feels the coin from Austin. He takes it out and inspects it as he asks, "What do you know about this curse, Mrs. Y?"

"Ah, the Curse of the Red Sea. I told you in the park that we were on sacred ground. Whatever caused this must be made right, or it will continue to manifest itself generation after generation."

"Yeah, but how? My brother is ready to burn this city down, and he's right that we need to change everything about this place, but how?"

She wraps her hand around his and balls it into a fist.

"Reasonable understanding and facts. The truth," she says. "You don't know that you already know the answers you need to fight with."

VII

It's almost sundown when Gabe pulls into the parking space at their apartment complex. The news update on the radio has announced that the barrier from the curse would be gone in an hour and warned New Locale's residents one last time to stay indoors tonight. Gabe thinks about his brother and everyone else who's ignoring the warning and standing on the battlefield in the park right now, but he is more focused on the battle that awaits him upstairs. He decides to test the waters before he enters and sends a text message to see if it's safe to go in.

"I'm downstairs. Be up in a sec."

After a few moments for his phone to buzz with a reply, but it never does. He takes a deep breath, grabs the bag and the flowers he bought from Seven Corners, and heads out of the car. He reaches the door and knocks twice after remembering that he doesn't have his keys. A few moments pass and there's no answer. He pulls out his phone again to send another text and when he looks down, he sees the fake rock that he and Chanel hide their space key in next to the door. He picks up the key and quickly bursts into the apartment to find it empty.

"Cha," he calls once. There's no answer. "Chanel!"

Gabe drops the flowers on the counter to head for the bedroom, and he sees a note.

In pretty cursive handwriting the note reads, "If you find this, I was trying to find you. Come find me at the park. We'll fight together."

The bag in his hand falls to the floor with the note as he dashes for the door. He's downstairs in an instant and in the car even quicker as he backs out of the space and heads down the street.

Chanel is just walking up to the park when she sees the last of the sun's light setting behind her. Marcus and a few of his friends are getting out of their cars on the West side as the police exit their cars on the East. They walk past the oak-tree-lined sidewalk and step onto the grass.

Chanel runs up to the group. "Marcus," she calls. "Where's Gabe?"

Where Love Resides

"Oh he punked out, huh?" He shakes his head. "That's crazy, man. I just saw him too, but I see who's really got the balls in y'all's house. Don't worry about him. We're out here and we got something to prove."

"I'm *very* worried about him now," she admits. "I only came out here to be with him! Where did you see him at?"

"Man, y'all scary asses can have each other. He was at Seven Corners about twenty minutes ago, buying candy like a little—" He locks eyes with an officer from afar and proceeds to walk past her. "You should have listened to us before!" Marcus shouts towards the men in uniform. "Now we've got to show you that we matter!" He and the thirty-odd other men and women line up at the center of the park, fists raised, chanting, "Show them we matter! Show them we matter!"

Chanel turns away from the park and starts to head back in the direction she came from. More people are making their way to the park now, joining Marcus and his friends at the center of it all. Her eyes are alert and scan the streets as her feet move quickly on the sidewalk.

She can still hear Marcus yelling behind her. "Best believe that by the end of the night you *will* respect our lives

115

and our power," he bellows. "This is our city, just as much as it's yours, and we've got to protect it from the ones who ain't protecting us!"

"They're not listening," Officer Bailey informs the mayor as they stand in her foyer. "They've got just as many men as we do out there and it sounds like more are coming."

"Let's go." She slings her coat over her shoulders. "Drive me down there before it's too late. We've only got about thirty minutes before the sun sets."

"Mom, I can't let you—"

"We've got to fix your mistake and make this right! Now let's go."

Mayor Banks gets in the passenger side of the police car with Officer Bailey. She has Officer Creek follow them in another car for extra protection. Their side of the city flies past them, like a blur through the windows, as they quickly ride down East Main Street. When they approach the park, they see that the whole New Locale police force is lined up at the barrier, but they are far outnumbered by the militant residents who are ready to fight for the good they believe in.

Mayor Banks uses the car's megaphone and commands, "New Locale PD, put your weapons down! This is not your fight. Do not take action against the residents! We need both sides of this city to cooperate and come together to resolve this. Please!"

"It's too late for that now," Marcus yells. "Theo's already gone! Y'all need to see understand what you've done to us."

Gabe races down the street, gripping the steering wheel and tightening his fists as he maneuvers around the block. His mind is empty aside from the image of Chanel. The temples of his forehead throb, his heart beats at ten times the normal speed thinking about reaching her before anything happens. The car barrels down the road, but a couple of blocks away from the park, crowds of people begin to block his path.

"C'mon!" He shouts slamming his hand down on the horn.

It doesn't help. He puts the car in park and gets out, joining the mob around him. Swiveling his head around as he walks, he sees how dark it's getting. His body is on autopilot as he stands in the street and the faces of the men and women blur as they run past him murmuring with excitement about taking matters into their own hands with threats of revenge. He barely hears them as is ears are filled with a ringing noise that clouds his mind as his feet continue to move faster, taking him closer to the park.

"Chanel!" He calls out into the sea of faces, hoping one of them will answer. None does. His jog through the street becomes a brisk run as he frantically searches through faces around him. He shouts again, "Cha!"

"Gabe?"

He hears her voice from a distance. It's coming from somewhere behind him and as he stops to look for her he realizes he's run too far down when he sees Marcus in the park, just as he douses a white T-shirt in lighter fluid.

"Gabe!" He hears her voice again.

He looks in the direction of her voice and in the middle of the swarm of people off in the distance he sees her. He's already running before he even has a chance to think about it. She catches sight of him as he runs and she begins taking slow, careful steps in his direction without taking her eyes off of him.

"Chanel, I'm coming!" Gabe cries out and dashes through the crowd.

Their eyes are locked as their bodies move towards each other, while in the park, the barrier begins to dissipate and bring the raging energies of East and West together. The officers stand strong, ready for battle, as the dozens of young citizens are poised with their purpose. Gabe holds out his arms to grab Chanel just before he reaches her. The moment their hands touch, Marcus pulls back his arm with the flaming shirt in his hand hurls it into the air. The fireball flies across the park, meeting the last of the barrier just before it disappears, causing it to explode with a violent blast that engulfs the park, then ripples through the rest of the town, setting the sky above them all ablaze. The blast knocks Chanel off her feet and Gabe dives down to her side. From the ground they see that though the sun has set, the sky has turned a bright orange as a rain of fire pours down and lightning strikes down from the clouds. The full wrath of the curse has found New Locale.

Gabe rises off the ground and pulls Chanel up with him, holding her hand in his as they run.

"We've gotta get to the car so we can get home," he tells her.

"Home?" She snatches her hand out of his and stands in the street. "We need to go to the church. Travis sent out a text saying they need all hands on deck for some safety zone they're making there tonight."

He stops to look at her with raised eyebrows and snaps, "You're texting Travis? And trusting him over *me*? Hell no, I'm not taking you over there! You see what happened to his *best friend* on his watch? As crazy as it is out here, we need to get home fast!"

"I'll stay out here then!" She whips her head around to walk back to the park. "I told you I won't let your negativity affect me!"

He presses the palm of his hand against his forehead as he speaks, trying to remain composed.

"Chanel, I'm trying to protect you that's all," he says calmly. "We can't help anyone if we die out here!"

"You're not going to keep holding me back from the things I'm trying to do, Gabe!" she snarls. "I made it home from the church on my own once. I'm sure I can make it back to the church on my own too!"

"Cha, please! This isn't the time for this," he yells.

"Why not? Because you say so," she says walking away. "It's time I have a say so about things and I'll show you that you need to listen one way or—"

"Chanel!" Gabe shouts.

He races over and tackles her to the ground just in time to avoid a fiery branch from the tree above them that collapses onto the ground where she was standing. He throws her over his shoulder, and runs the rest of the way to the car. He opens the door and drops her into the passenger seat before he slams it shut.

"You said the church is the safe zone?" he asks.

With her arms crossed and head turned, staring out the window, she dryly replies, "Yeah."

He turns the key and revs the engine before he swerves the car around to head down the street.

"Look," he starts, "you can be mad at me all you want, tomorrow or whenever all this is over. But right now, I need you to work with me. I can see that we won't be able to make it to the apartment, so I'm heading to the church. You're getting your way, regardless of my wishes, so I'm willing to listen to you." He turns to face her. "Can we call a truce for now so we can get through this?"

"Gabe!" she shouts, pointing at the two flaming police cars cross in front of them, blocking the road he was turning onto.

"*Shit!*"

121

He jerks the car to a stop, and they sit there for a moment as he contemplates his next move. Chanel notices the wide-eyed, uneasy expression on his face and melts her stiff attitude.

"All right, truce," she says. "Try the detour street by Seven Corners to get there. That's out the way so there shouldn't be too many people on it."

Without a moment's notice, he swings the car around to head down West Main Street. His alert eyes scan the night roads. He maneuvers through the abandoned cars, flaming debris, and obstacles in their path. Just when they thought they'd gotten past the worst of it and road seemed clear, Gabe brings the car to a screeching stop as a man jumps out of the bushes and runs past, screaming with his arms flailing in the air and entire body covered in fire. Gabe bursts out of the car to help the man, looking for something to put out the flames, but his empty hands are no good, so he stands frozen in shock, unsure of what to do.

"Hey!" Chanel calls out to stop a police officer who was running behind their car and points at the man.

He runs over and wraps his body around the man before they roll onto to the ground. Chanel grabs Gabe's hand and drags him back to the car. He continues down the road just in time to notice Mrs. Yamassee standing outside of the Seven Corners store, flagging them down for help. Gabe makes a hard turn to pull into the lot and the two of them erupt from the car to meet her.

"Oh Gabe, Chanel, please come this way, quick!" she cries. She leads them to the back of the store and explains, "We got locked out of the store and two children showed up. One of them has a badly hurt leg."

They make it to the back but are blocked by a wall of fire that stops them. Gabe lifts a fire extinguisher from the wall next to them and sprays it, revealing six old women huddled in a circle over two boys, protecting them from the fire. Mrs. Yamassee joins them, and Gabe is still as he sees all seven of the women in the flesh at once. He quickly snaps out of it as one of the boys calls out his name, and he realizes that it's Austin and his friend from earlier.

"Gabe!" the boy calls out enthusiastically. "Me and Donny were trying to cross to the East side to find my dad, but we had to run from the explosion, and I tripped and fell on my knee."

"Please take them somewhere safe," Mrs. Yamassee asks.

Gabe quickly picks up Austin and heads back to the car as Chanel leads Donny behind them. She stops and turns.

123

"Wait. What about you all, Mrs.—"

Gabe looks behind him to face the women, but they are gone.

"I told you. Witches!" he shouts as they run.

They get to the car, strap the boys in the seatbelts of the backseat, and continue their drive to the church. As they get closer to the park where the explosion erupted, the chaos and fire thicken and intensify. More people cross their path, people from all sides of the city, many hurt or trying by any means to escape harm's way. Gabe dodges and swerves to avoid them, demonstrating lightning-fast agility and skill as he drives.

"Mr. Gabe," Austin says.

Gabe silently continues his maneuvering, so Chanel turns around to answer the child.

"Gabe's a little busy, Austin," she says in a soothing voice. "What do you need?"

"Oh, Mr. Gabe's wife," he says as if pleased to meet her. "Where are we going? Can we go to find my dad, please?"

"We're trying to get to the church at the end of the park," she informs him. "That's where we'll be safe until things are better, and then we can go find your dad, okay? And you can call me Ms. Chanel."

"Um, Ms. Chanel," Donny says in a shy, quiet voice. "Do you and Mr. Gabe have any kids?"

She laughs and replies, "Oh, no. Not right now. Why do you ask?"

"I was wondering," he answers, "Since you're going to help Austin get to his dad, and my parents have been gone for a long time, can you two adopt me?"

"Hey, Donny," Gabe interjects. "I don't want to be rude, but let's worry about saving our lives first, before we make any long-term plans. We're all family in this car right now. I haven't even checked on my own brother who could be—"

"Oh my God! There's Marcus!" Chanel points.

In the middle of the park, Marcus stands with a gun in his hand, aimed right at Officer Bailey, who has his hands raised above him.

"*Daddy*!" Austin cries.

VIII

"*Daddy?*" both Gabe and Chanel gasp, snapping their heads around to look at Austin.

Gabe just shakes his head and leaps out of the car.

"Marcus!" he yells. He stomps through the flames on the ground as he races across the tree-lined sidewalk and onto the park grass toward his brother at the center of the park. "Marcus, no!"

Reverend Brown and Travis are standing with him as Marcus, who turns to see Gabe coming their way.

"Oh, look, Bailey," Marcus says, gripping the gun with both hands and aiming right at the officer's head. "Now you have to face both sons of the man you killed before you die."

"Marcus, don't do this," Gabe says as he reaches them.

"It was an accident!" Officer Bailey pleads, his hands shaking. "I shot the wrong man." He is flushed red and the veins on his forehead bulge like his eyes as he admits his mistake. "I shot your father instead of the suspect at the bank. He was running to catch the thief himself when I…" He hangs his head to the ground. "The guy got away and took off in a car that killed my son, who was playing in this park. I never forgave myself for it." He falls to his knees. "I'm sorry. It's hurt us both."

Mayor Banks stands behind him, holding her hands to her chest, while Officer Creek stands armed and ready with his gun aimed at Marcus.

"Oh, I'm doing it!" Marcus warns. "I told you, I'm a New Locale soldier. I'll risk it all for my people."

"No, you don't have to do this!" Gabe shouts.

Marcus turns to Gabe in confusion, keeping the gun raised with one hand.

"What do you mean? This man killed our father! He's killed Theo! Are we going to wait for him to take the next innocent man's life? 'Cause I'm not!"

"And that man behind him is ready to take your life as soon as you pull that trigger," Gabe argues. "C'mon, man. Mom left, Dad is gone. I can't bear to lose you too."

"Look, I gotta do what I gotta do to make this right."

Chanel is walking up with Donnie beside her, carrying Austin on her back. Officer Bailey looks behind Marcus and catches a glimpse of his son.

"Austin," he whispers. "My boy…"

"*Oh!* This is your son?" His face lights up as he cackles a sinister laugh and taunts, "Now your son has to watch you die!" Marcus yells. "You did this to yourself."

"Marcus!" Gabe cries.

He feels a burning in his pocket and grabs at it to find the coin from Austin has turned a fiery red again. It scorches his fingers and he tosses it in the air just as Marcus squeezes the trigger, and the officer behind them does the same. The two bullets fly through the air, right at each other, the coin flips in between them. They all smack into each other causing that same blue wave of light to emerge from the collision as the barrier erupts from the ground again.

"Man, forget this!" Marcus yells, tossing the gun to the ground as he storms off.

"Daddy," Austin calls from behind Chanel.

"Austin, please come here!" Bailey cries.

"I can't walk, Daddy," the child says. "I need someone to help me cross over."

Everyone looks around at each other. Gabe hears his father's voice telling him the story of the curse from when he was a boy.

"There's a trick to it," Moses says in his memory. "Any child can cross over if they haven't been taught to hate. But the grown folks, they must decide to move with the purest of intentions or be drowned in the waters of God's wrath."

Gabe walks over to Chanel.

"Let me carry him," he says.

"Gabe," she says with worried eyes. "Are you sure?"

He pauses, then nods. "I can't respect any of the things this man has done as an officer. I'm feel utter disgust at the chaos he's cast upon my home so many times. But," he says, taking Austin in his arms, "his son has come back from the other side for a reason. I only wish I had the chance to see my father again, and for Austin's sake *only*, I don't want to rob him of the chance to be reunited with his dad."

Chanel's eyes well up with tears. Reverend Brown places his hand on Gabe's shoulder and gives him a firm squeeze with a hopeful smile.

Gabe takes two steps forward and stops in front of the barrier. Officer Bailey, still on his knees, gazes up with tears

129

rolling down his face. Gabe looks down at Austin, who gives him a smile. Everyone holds their breath as Gabe closes his eyes and places one foot into the wave. He opens his eyes and exhales a breath of relief as he sets it on the ground on the other side. He with joy as he continues to cross over, but as he moves further into the wave, Austin's body begins to glow into a blindingly bright white light. Officer Bailey jumps up to grab his son, but before he can reach him, the boy's body dissolves and breaks off into particles of light that float away into the air.

"Austin, no!" Bailey wails at the sight of his son slipping away once again.

Everyone stands with mouths agape as they look to the sky to see Austin leave.

"That means he's crossed for good," says Donny. "I've been trying to cross over. I miss my mom and dad."

Officer Bailey, with tears running down his face, looks over at the other child.

"Donny? Donny Carmichael?" he asks wiping his eyes. "Do you remember me?"

Donny regards him, still with fear, before his face breaks into a bright-eyed smile.

"Brandon!" he exclaims. "You're old now!"

"How did you cross over? How long have you been here?"

"I've been here a long time. Since I got hung from the rope on the tree over there." Donny points in the direction of the mayor's home. "I was by myself until Austin came. He was my new best friend, just like you were!"

"Mom." Bailey twists around "Didn't you say Donny moved away? That Dad left because of him?"

All eyes are on Mayor Banks as they wait for her to answer.

"I told you…" she starts, her face stern and her tone unapologetic. "Your father did what he had to do to fix his mistake. We thought your friend had stolen money from our house, and well… that was our first time seeing the curse. Your father gave himself up to break it." She shrugs, "So, in a way he did leave because of Donny."

"I didn't steal anything!" Donny shouts, charging forward into the barrier, and instantly dissolving the way Austin had before him.

"Mom, how could you…" Bailey trails off. "You've let me live thinking…"

As if lost, he begins to pace around in a daze.

The mayor wraps her arms around him in an embrace that is perhaps more for her benefit than his. "Oh, Brandon," she starts, "it all worked out in the end, didn't it? Look at where it got us. It helped me to start my climb into city politics, and I know you don't think that your careless incompetence is what kept you on the police force, do you? You're lucky these boys stayed quiet when Mrs. Mathis took the hush money and moved away for you too."

"Gabe?" Chanel asks bearing an expression of shock and confusion.

He looks at her with remorseful eyes. "We were kids. We didn't know how to fight, and this place was all we knew. We stayed here and, like she said, we stayed quiet."

Bailey pushes his mother away, causing her to lose her balance. As she stumbles backwards, she falls into the barrier wave. Shaking violently from head to toe, a red light pours out from every inch of her skin as she sinks into the ground, disappearing from right before their eyes. Everyone freezes in silence on both sides of the barrier.

"Why isn't it gone?" Gabe asks. "She's the one who caused all of this. That makes it right now, doesn't it?"

Reverend Brown speaks up. "It has to be the person who killed Theo." He fixed Bailey with a firm look.

Officer Bailey walks over to the barrier, then turns to Gabe.

"I know there's nothing that I can do or say to make up for what I've done," he tells him, "but I can only hope that had I known what I know now, maybe things here could've been different."

Gabe listens, then gives him a single nod of his head, respecting and appreciating the apologetic nature of his words.

Officer Bailey steps into the barrier, and as his body reflects that bright light, the waves condense and collapse into him. Bailey dissolves along with the barrier, and the city is one again. All of those standing there began to clap and cheer. Gabe runs over to Chanel to hold her in his arms and embrace her.

IX

Holding Chanel's face in his hands, Gabe stares lovingly into her eyes.

"Thank you," he tells her. "To think I wanted us to go home. You're the reason we're going to move forward now." He gently plants a kiss on her forehead.

"Gabe", she starts, her eyes welling up with tears, "I was so worried about you. I thought you'd gone out to fight, and all I wanted was to come out here and fight with you. To do whatever we had to do to let the past, your father—" She presses her hand on his cheek. "To let all of it guide us into the future. But this…" She pauses. "Thank you. I-I don't even know what to say except I love you so much."

"I'm so sorry, babe," he says. "I was wrong about how I acted today, dismissing your views, taking you for granted. I'm so sorry."

"No, Gabe. I'm sorry. I'm always thinking about how to make things better for everyone else, how to fix the damage that's been done around us, I wasn't even thinking about what you've been through here and how I can help you. I should've listened to you."

He hushes her. "*Shhh...* I don't want to fight about who was wrong or not. I want you to show me your vision. I want to give you my understanding and I want you to help me see the good you're trying to create so that I can do what I can to support you. I want to build the good here. I want to believe in you. I want to be better for you. I need you, Chanel," he says, grabbing her waist. "I need all of you with me forever, okay?"

Chanel's eyes glow in awe. "Are you kidding?" she gushes. "I haven't seen a better Gabe! You've been so brave. I know your dad is proud," she looks into the sky. "I'm proud of how you protected Austin. And what you did for Bailey? Nothing less than heroic, babe."

"Nah," Marcus interrupts. "That bully Bailey, should've stayed here to tell everyone what really happened! You think they're going to believe any of *us* if we try to tell the truth?"

"They have to believe us," Travis says. "We have proof!"

He raises the cellphone in his hand and they see the camera light on, as it's recording everything.

Gabe moves to join Travis. "C'mon, man! That's what I'm talking about!" He extends his arm and the two of them clasp hands in a firm, dapping handshake. "We need to get this heard ASAP. Bailey might be right—things could be different here if we knew the truth."

Travis snaps his fingers and says, "Theo's radio show!" He puts the phone to his ear. "I'm calling to tell them you're coming to plug this into the station signal. We'll get the word out so everyone hears it before it goes off. What time is it?"

"A quarter to ten," Chanel answers.

"The show ends at ten," Travis informs. He pauses, and they hear the automated message on the other end. "No answer, but the show is on auto-play tonight. You gotta get there quick and get this on. We need to get as many people listening as possible!"

"I can get to the police station and use our tower to broadcast the signal," offers Officer Creek.

"I'll get back to the church and play it for everyone there," says Reverend Brown.

"Let me get my girls to tell their friends, to tell their friends," Marcus suggests with a sneaky grin.

Gabe nods to Chanel, and they take off for the car.

"Cha," he says, "I need you to drive, and fast. The station is at the end of West Main."

"Let's go," she replies, already putting the car in gear.

He flips on the radio, and sure enough, they hear Theo's voice.

"I just wanted to say, that even though it seems like my life or the lives of my brothers and sisters before me don't matter, I think we all have the power to do something, anything, to change that," he is saying.

The car clock reads 9:42 PM. They have to get through what was left of the riot and reach the radio station. Chanel, focused and determined, pushes the pedal down and the car steadily eases along the street. Officer Creek is approaching the police station on the other side, the church was already listening to the show, and Marcus has sent the first chain of text messages from his phone.

They all hear Theo as he continues saying, "I always thought that I would have to do everything alone, that no one would listen to me. I'm grateful for my friends and family,

137

who believed and supported me from the beginning, and for the rare, nature of my friend, my brother, Travis. He's seen life on both sides of New Locale and his willingness to give help in whatever way he can makes me know that *all of us* have some way that we can help in this mission…"

Gabe and Chanel are passing City Hall, and the radio station is just around the corner. The tires screech on the worn pavement as she makes a hard turn to stop the car in front of the radio station door. Gabe is halfway out the door, but he stops and leans over to kiss Chanel before he goes in. She smiles as he pulls away and runs up the front steps. He yanks on the door, but it's locked. He quickly races around the building, but the back door is locked too. The time on the phone and it reads 9:54 PM. He scans the area with his alert eyes and spots a fire escape ladder. Securing the phone in his pocket, he jumps onto it and begins to climb.

As he makes his way up, step by step, he hears Theo's closing remarks. "It doesn't matter how big or small the impact of our actions might be. What matters is that we do *something*. Something to change the way things are, to make this world better, to give back in honor of the ones who gave their all before us, and to make things fair for the ones who will come after us. Spreading the truth of these words so we can conquer the unjust hate, and make this a place where love resides. That's all I got y'all…"

At the top of the building, Gabe sees the station's satellite. He unlocks the phone, which now reads 9:58 PM, and starts the playback of the video. But there is nowhere to hook the phone into the tower! Gabe howls with frustration. Then, in a moment of faith, he draws his arm back and casts the phone into the satellite dish. The phone just barely lands on its rim, and as the tower begins to tremble, a blue electric current builds up from the base until it shoots out of the antennae into the sky.

Backing away, Gabe gazes looks out over the city, and everywhere he sees small streams of blue light rising from the houses, cars, and phones of the residents of New Locale, collecting in the clouds and pouring down like an electric rain. He sees the flames of hate being extinguished across the city, as the truth is revealed for all who live there.

<u>Epilogue</u>

Gabe and Chanel leave the doctor's office, ready to meet their friends and so they can share the news. In their car, Gabe sits in the passenger seat, a smile on his face, reclining with his left hand behind his head as he plots ideas in the notebook labeled "The Mathis' Vision Journal". Chanel sits upright in the driver's seat, her belly just inches from the steering wheel as she eases the car out of the parking lot, onto East Main Street. Gabe clicks the radio on.

"Good afternoon, New Locale!" DJ MMS calls with glee from the radio. "It's a beautiful day today, isn't it? The sun is shining bright as ever, there's not a single cloud in the sky, and the music is good, as usual, right?" She laughs. "I got a request from Reverend—excuse me," she corrects, "that's Mayor Brown now, who asked me to spin this one to congratulate our city's favorite couple on the new addition to their family. Here's Stevie Wonder's 'As' for you, Gabe and Chanel."

The sunlight hits the gold paint of the car, and Gabe looks out of the window as they pass City Hall and approach Central Park. He marvels at the statue erected in the middle of the field. A stone frame with arrows extending from the top out to the East and to the West stand some twenty feet in the air, allow any person to walk through from either side as commemoration of the day the Curse of the Red Sea was broken.

"What do you think about getting a place close to here?" he asks.

Chanel pauses for a moment before she replies in a teasing voice, "What, you want *my* opinion?" They laugh and she says, "You know I'm still getting used to this new Gabe. Being over here would be new, something different."

"Well, I was thinking," he says. "With you starting the new community coordinator job at the center, and since I'm working at the police station now, it'd be better for us to be closer to the East side. And there's so much history here." He looks at a group of kids running through the statue. "'*Nah kuh chah kih*', like Mrs. Y says. I want our baby to be close to the sacred energy that surrounds us."

She looks over at him and smiles. "I think that sounds beautiful," she says. "They'll know that their father is the hero who changed the city."

"Yeah, and don't forget you were with me then, inspiring my heart to do it, too."

They arrive at a newly constructed two-story brick building that sits on the southeast end of the park just next to the church. Sleek metallic letters over the doors read "Theophilus Monroe Community Center", and at the steps in front of it sits Travis and Marcus, waiting to greet them.

"Wassup!" Marcus says with a smile. He opens his arms to give Chanel a big hug before he daps Gabe's hands before he asks the question. "So what's the word? Boy or girl?"

Gabe checks with Chanel, who nods and grins. "We'll be bringing little Moses Theophilus Mathis into the world this May," he announces.

"*Yesssss!*" Marcus leaps up, throwing his fist in the air. "Oh, my lil nephew is about to be the freshest, flyest kid to ever hit these New Locale streets! Well, after me of course," he says pulling up on his shirt collar.

"Congrats, man," Travis says giving Gabe a pat on the back. "Moses T! Theo would love it."

"It's our way of honoring him," Chanel tells him. "It's crazy that they hid the news about everything from the mainstream. Of course the standard police report is out, and that's all the world will know about Theo, but..." She shakes her head.

"We know the truth," Gabe adds. "We won't forget."

The four of them walk into the building, and its rooms are filled with the residents of New Locale, from every age, race, and walk of life. In this center they talk and teach lessons to build a future together from the past they've shared. Theo is gone from the physical world, but he lives on in the hearts and minds of his friends, and all the residents of this small town, so that even as it begins to change, his story and legacy are at the core of every thought, feeling, and action that takes place from here on. Their love for him grows from reasonable understanding grounded in the truth, and blossoms everyday into a love for all that reside in that small city in Southern Georgia.

Author's Note

The preceding text is a fictional account of a fictional city that reflects on a very real issue plaguing our society. As of late, it seems that police brutality is not in the major headlines of the news, but this is something that lurks and hides in the shadows of our history and, like a recurring curse, waits to manifest itself causing a continuous pattern of hate and division in our communities. This narrative is my way of asking us all to look at the life and the histories we've been told to be true and dig deeper. We often look at this as a racial issue, as it is on the surface, but looking into the stories that we available online, I found that this issue was happening in communities of all demographics. This is a moral issue of abuse of power that is at the root of many forms of injustices, and has been overlooked and tolerated by our leaders in inexcusable ways. I urge you to find a list of all the lives that have been taken due to police, as Travis did, and as I have, since the death of Trayvon Martin. His was the first high profile case I was old enough to recall and, unfortunately as you will see, very far from the last. The information shocked me into a realization that the news we hear is in most cases not the *full* truth. The discovery of one truth almost always leads to another, and another, until the depth of deception that lies in our understandings of life will be revealed. With this information, do as you must, as I too will continue my Life's mission to use my words to spread Love for all, create Peace by any means necessary, and share Light through knowledge. Thank you.

Ashley.

ABOUT THE AUTHOR

Ashley A.T. is a writer based out of Atlanta, GA. Born and raised just outside of Miami, FL, as a child, Ashley was always highly creative and took rigorous classes that allowed her to learn to write extensively about a variety of subjects. The oldest of two girls, her father, a now retired officer of the military, and her mother, an experienced educator, both encouraged and helped their girls to achieve academic success and develop their personal talents. As a hopeless romantic, Ashley used writing to express the emotions she would feel while falling in and out of love. In college, she discovered a new outlet for her writing abilities after joining the journalism club and writing for the college newspaper, as well as digging into her roots after taking a student intern job at the John G. Riley Center/Museum of African American History and Culture.

As Ashley continued her education, taking IT courses and electives with a focus on the arts stimulated her passion for writing through assignments where she wrote essays, articles, analyses about different subjects and through various creative expressions. Through her love of music, Ashley began to take interest in the poetic nature of songwriting, and started writing poetry her senior year of college, and has since acquired an online following after sharing her poems about love and life. After graduating and moving to Atlanta for an IT job, Ashley A.T. released her poetry collection, the well-received, passionately insightful *The Lotus' Love Suite*. Since then, Ashley's views and understanding of the world continued to expand, and aligning with the principles of Universal Love, she was inspired to write a series of novels that address issues of social justice and acceptance, starting with *Where Love Resides*. Ashley is breaking into the urban writing scene and inspiring a new generation of readers, writing from the heart with a mission and a message to spread Love, Peace, and Light.

HAVE YOU READ?

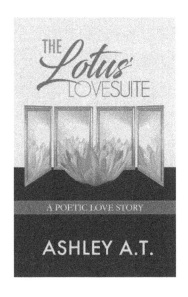

The Lotus' Love Suite
– Ashley A.T.'s poetic
novella explores the
depths of love in a story
about a relationship that
inspires a great
transformation through
the highs and lows of
the journey that reflects
light and inspires others
to discover their own
transformation.

Visit www.Ashley-AT.com to order
your copy today.

@_OfTheAshTree

Skin Deep by *Ashley A.T.*

In the eyes of God, you and I both see the same Sun shining.
So how can I look at you and not see a reflection of me?
From a love for me, I found a love for all that resides in we
Looking past the things that separate us from each other
physically
Like being born into bodies, assigned skin tones and nationalities
that divide the he and she
Confining us to communities united by a lack of unity
And distracting us with all that blinds us of our inner beauty.

So, I've decided to embrace the soul in all of us living things
Ignoring the exterior discrepancies that hide what connects us
underneath
Like the light that shines down from His love for you and me
Where the things that unite us lie beyond where the eyes can see
And because of that, the love I have for us is
beyond skin deep.

Where Love Resides Synopsis

Gabe Mathis was not prepared for the tragedy that would strike his small town of New Locale, Georgia that warm Autumn night. There had been tragedies before, and there would surely be more to follow, but, this one… This was the one that would change history. The people of that slow-paced city in the deep south, would find themselves instantly propelled into a destiny that would change, not only their lives, but the entire world.

The killing of 22-year-old, Theophilus Monroe III, better known as Theo, and New Locale's town hero, split the city in two. Setting off a chain reaction of events, the people would be forced to find and accept a dark secret from their city's past, change the way newlyweds, Gabe and Chanel, find love in their home, and made all of them watch hate start vicious fire that would come to cleanse their city if they could not find peace before it was too late.

As Gabe and Chanel, along with their friends, family, and community, stand on different sides in the battle for justice for their fallen hero, and the powers that be do all that they can to prevent a truth that would turn the city on itself from being revealed, all would discover if this is truly a city where love resides.

CPSIA information can be obtained
at www.ICGtesting.com
Printed in the USA
FSHW011342010919
61580FS